"I wanted to be your wife, Leon. I still do,"

Cassie said softly.

"Well, that's what you are," he said, "legally, anyway."

That was like a physical blow. She caught her breath. "I want to go on being your wife," she said quietly, "in every way."

He looked up sharply. "You'd do just about anything for your boys, wouldn't you?"

She blanched. "Not that! I—I want that for *me!*"

"And what do you want for me, Cassie?"

"I want everything good for you. You deserve it."

"Gratitude!" he spat, suddenly angry.

"Then just tell me what you want, Leon," she implored him.

His eyes were hard and flashing. "There are some things that just can't be had for the asking, Cassie. You can't manufacture feelings that aren't there."

She stiffened. He didn't want her anymore, and there was nothing either one of them could do about it.

Dear Reader,

This month, Silhouette Romance brings you six wonderful new love stories—guaranteed to keep your summer sizzling! Starting with a terrific FABULOUS FATHER by Arlene James. A *Mail-order Brood* was not what Leon Paradise was expecting when he asked Cassie Esterbridge to be his wife. So naturally the handsome rancher was shocked when he discovered that his mail-order bride came with a ready-made family!

Favorite author Suzanne Carey knows the kinds of stories Romance readers love. And this month, Ms. Carey doesn't disappoint. *The Male Animal* is a humorous tale of a couple who discover love—in the midst of their divorce.

The fun continues as Marie Ferrarella brings us another delightful tale from her Baby's Choice series—where matchmaking babies bring together their unsuspecting parents.

In an exciting new trilogy from Sandra Steffen, the Harris brothers vow that no woman will ever tie them down. But their WEDDING WAGER doesn't stand a chance against love. This month, a confirmed bachelor suddenly becomes a single father—and a more-than-willing groom—in *Bachelor Daddy*.

Rounding out the month, Jeanne Rose combines the thrill of the chase with the excitement of romance in *Love on the Run*. And *The Bridal Path* is filled with secrets—and passion—as Alaina Hawthorne spins a tale of love under false pretenses.

I hope you'll join us in the coming months for more great books from Elizabeth August, Kasey Michaels and Helen Myers.

Until then—

Happy Reading!

Anne Canadeo
Senior Editor

Please address questions and book requests to:
Silhouette Reader Service
U.S.: 3010 Walden Ave., P.O. Box 1325, Buffalo, NY 14269
Canadian: P.O. Box 609, Fort Erie, Ont. L2A 5X3

MAIL-ORDER BROOD

Arlene James

Silhouette
R O M A N C E™
Published by Silhouette Books
America's Publisher of Contemporary Romance

 SILHOUETTE BOOKS

ISBN 0-373-19024-7

MAIL-ORDER BROOD

Copyright © 1994 by Arlene James

This edition published by arrangement with Harlequin Enterprises B. V.

Printed in U.S.A.

ARLENE JAMES

grew up in Oklahoma and has lived all over the South. In 1976, she married "the most romantic man in the world." The author enjoys traveling with her husband, but writing has always been her chief pastime.

Leon Paradise on Fatherhood...

I'm not the first old boy in this particular part of the country to get a wife through a personal advertisement. But there are pitfalls, for sure.

In this case, I thought I was getting a wife, but what I wound up with is a whole brood of boys! Six, to be exact. Now I don't know what I'm going to do. I wanted Cassie, wanted her enough to take on her young son with her. But I didn't know when I put that ring on her finger that I was putting my neck in a noose of her making! Now I have to wonder if I'll ever get it out again.

See, it's not the boys' fault. They're scamps, right enough, but even a scamp deserves a safe, nurturing home. And a loving father, which I think I could try my doggone best to be. But one way or another I have to know what's in Cassie's heart, or we've got no chance at all of being a family, and that's a pure shame, it surely is. Because I tell you what, 20,000 acres never looked so big to me before—or so lonely.

Wish me luck, pard. With this bunch I'll definitely need it!

Chapter One

Cassie woke to the drone of diesel engines and the smell of stale cigarette smoke. She sat up straight and gritted her teeth against the pain of a crick in her neck. She had thought that the bus trip would be an adventure, but so far nothing was working out as she'd hoped. Her throat ached from the tears she'd shed at leaving her loved ones behind in West Virginia, and her eyes stung from cigarette smoke and lack of sleep. Leaving West Virginia had been surprisingly difficult. Saying goodbye to the boys and Petey had been one of the hardest things she'd ever done. Dear Petey. He had stared up at her with those wide, trusting eyes, his small hand grasped tightly in Dodie's, and smiled through the confusion clouding his little face. She had promised him fervently that they would be together again soon, and he had given her a nod, his eyes swimming with tears. It had almost been a relief to turn away and board the bus, but then to see them all standing there together, the hope shining in their faces as they waved and smiled bravely, had brought a lump to her throat and an ache in her chest.

She closed her eyes and prayed. This had to work. It simply could not be a mistake, for there was no going back, nothing to go back to, only doing without and being unwelcome. In Texas she could have a husband and a home again. In Texas she and the boys would be safe, unless ... But no, she wouldn't think like that. Leon Paradise had been kind enough to send the bus fare, kind enough to write her all those months, and kind enough not to ask too many questions when she'd first refused, then changed her mind and accepted his invitation to come to Texas. Perhaps he would not be all that Jos had been, but he need not be what her father was, either.

Advertising for a wife might be a strange way to get one in this day and time, but it took more character and courage than seducing a seventeen-year-old and getting her pregnant. Not that her "stepmother" could be called innocent by any means. Marlene was, in her way, as bad as Chintz Esterbridge was in his. They were a matched set, those two, one spoiled and smug and manipulative, the other selfish and bullying. Together they had made her life and the lives of her young son and brothers a living hell. Whatever she was going to, it could not be much worse than what she'd come from. If it wasn't what she'd had with Jos, either, well, a woman didn't get that lucky twice in a lifetime, and she always had Petey, Jos's son.

But she was getting way ahead of herself here. Leon Paradise might not even want her when all was said and done, especially when she told him about the boys, *if* she told him about the boys. It might not even get that far.

"I'm not a lonely man," he had written. "I'll admit I have my lonesome moments, living out here all by myself in the middle of twenty thousand acres, but I wouldn't change this life I lead. I love it out here. I love ranching. Some folks look around them in this place and just see desert rimmed by rocky mountains, but I see freedom and the West and being my own man in the way generations of cowboys have been in the past. No, I'm not a lonely man, but I do want a wife, a partner, someone to share all this with. I think we ought to find out if that's you.''

A wife, a partner, someone to share with. Cassie turned to stare at her reflection in the window. Could that be her? Would he still feel that way when he met her? She didn't see anything in her face to suggest a man would lose all sense and fall at her feet in a stupor. It was just a face, kind of plain, nothing remarkable about it, wide at the top, narrow at the bottom, with two largish eyes, a middle-of-the-road nose and a mouth that wasn't too large or too small. Her hair was ash blond, straight as a board, and cropped just below the nape of her neck. If there was anything remarkable about her at all, it was the color of her eyes. Esterbridge green, the folks at home in the hills of West Virginia called it, but she didn't see that it was all that arresting, especially as Chintz had them, too. No, she didn't see anything there to make Leon Paradise think that he had to have her, especially as she came with six boys.

Would he even have written her the first time if her friend Dodie had told him about the boys when she'd answered his ad on Cassie's behalf? She couldn't believe he would have. A man might have taken on one child without too much resentment. If he really loved a woman, he might even take on two. But six? No man in his right mind would take on six boys. And no woman in her right mind would expect him to. But what choice did she have? Chintz and Marlene had made it clear that they wanted Cassie and the boys out of the house before the new baby came. She'd looked for work, hoping to find something that would make it possible for her to support the seven of them, but the hills of West Virginia did not abound in employment opportunities, certainly not the kind that would allow a widowed mother with only a G.E.D. to keep a roof over the heads of seven people. That high school diploma had seemed so unimportant when she'd married Josiah Hunter at sixteen. Jos had taken her away from her father's house and provided her a loving home, and he'd given her Petey, and she had thought that life would be wonderful from that point on. Then Jos had died in that mining accident, and she had discovered that even a newly acquired G.E.D. could not open doors where there were no doors to be opened.

The only way out she'd seen in a very long time now was the one opened for her by Leon Paradise. Since Chintz had put her and Petey out of his house, she had no choice but to walk through that door to Leon, and it was just a matter of time before her young brothers would be in that same position. If she didn't find a way to provide for them, they'd be absorbed by the welfare system, the younger four, anyway, and she feared that she would never see them again. Dodie had convinced her that Leon Paradise was heaven sent, that it was fated that he and Cassie should team up and that she had known it since the moment she'd read his personal advertisement in back of a horse breeder's magazine left on one of the benches at her little combination store and bus stop. Over the months, as Leon's simple, oddly eloquent letters had revealed a hardworking cowboy with the soul of a poet, Dodie had declared Cassie a fool for not jumping at the opportunity he offered her. She'd even gone so far as to declare that she'd head to West Texas herself if only she was closer to fifty than seventy. But Dodie had also counseled her not to mention the boys. "Give it a chance," she'd said. "Just see what develops first."

It hadn't seemed so deceptive when Cassie had had no intention of becoming a modern version of a mail-order bride. Now it seemed not only deceptive but shameful, almost criminal. And yet she couldn't see a way to go back. All she could do was go forward and hope that Leon liked her well enough to overlook the small matter of six boys to raise, five, really. At nineteen Newt was practically an adult, and, too, she had to remember that Petey wouldn't be any trouble for anyone. He was such a quiet, shy four-year-old. Now Freddy was hardly shy, but his sense of humor was well developed for a seven-year-old, and he could certainly be an entertaining little scamp. At ten, Bart considered himself above Freddy's silly antics, but the two of them were as close as could be. Before Bart had gotten his glasses, Freddy had led him around by the hand and run interference for him with the other kids. If Freddy occasionally took advantage of Bart's inability to see clearly, well it seemed a fair trade-off. The twins, Kyler and Kole, for all their mischief, had never teased Bart about his vision problems, either, but at fourteen, she had to admit they were a handful. They needed guidance, though, not brutality, which was Chintz's way of dealing with their little larks. Dodie felt certain that Leon Paradise would provide that guidance, and at the time Cassie had concurred. But now, in the dark of night with Van Horn, Texas, and the moment of meeting coming up fast, she had to wonder if she hadn't made a mistake.

It wouldn't work. It couldn't. He was going to take one look and put her on the next bus heading east. Or he was going to turn out to be a smooth talker like Chintz with no real essence to him. Maybe he'd even turn mean when he found out about the boys. And maybe she wouldn't be able to go through with it even if he was Prince Charming himself—especially if he was Prince Charming. Yet, what choice would she have then that she didn't have now? No matter how she worked it around in her mind, she always came up against that same wall. He was the only chance she had. He was the only chance the boys had, and she knew, in her heart, that she'd do whatever she had to and hope for the best. One thing was certain, no matter what kind of man Leon Paradise revealed himself to be, if he could be brought to marry her, she would be the finest wife for whom any man could hope. That much she would do for her own self-respect but also because any man who would provide a home for her and her boys deserved as muc'

For comfort, she took Leon's letters from her purse and reread them in chronological order. They did much to calm her fears. No man who could write so simply but so lovingly of a land could be an unfeeling man. No man who could show such pride and take such pleasure in his work could be a weak man. No man who could so eloquently reach out to a stranger half a continent away could be a small man. Maybe it would be all right if he could just like her. That had to come first. Then, if it seemed they might suit, she could tell him about the boys. With that much settled in her mind, she carefully put away the letters, laid her head back and sought relief in sleep.

She had begun her journey in darkness, and she would end it the same way. Since Odessa she'd hardly been able to sit still, let alone rest. Determined to see something of the land about which Leon Paradise had written so passionately, she stared through the window, glimpsing in the almost impenetrable night the vague heaviness of distant mountains in every direction and the seemingly bare, flat, moon-washed stretches of the northern Chihuahua Desert between. It was unlike anything she had imagined. Deeply mysterious, cloaked in the heaviness of a night so black that the horizon could be distinguished only by the lack of stars, it seemed as limitless as the heavens. And such stars! She would not have believed the sky could hold them all. The vastness of them made her feel small and hidden, safe somehow. It was a feeling that would not last.

All too soon the mountains closed in around the wide ribbon of highway and then gave way to the lights of Van Horn which diminished the sky and concentrated her attention on the meeting to come. Her heart was pounding long before the bus exited the highway and made the turn that carried it through the sleeping town. It was something of a disappointment after the beckoning lights, for it seemed to consist of two intersecting roads and perhaps a dozen unpaved streets lined with blockish buildings that somehow all seemed deserted. Then suddenly the bus was squealing to a stop beside a dark cafe with an unpainted bench sitting against a side wall. The door hissed open, and Cassie's heart climbed into her throat.

The driver got off first, opened the luggage compartment, and lifted out her battered suitcase and a single cardboard box tied with twine. With a great force of will, Cassie got her feet beneath her, rose and carefully made her way down the aisle of the darkened bus, pausing at the door.

She was almost glad that the street was empty, though it made her arrival strangely anticlimactic. She took a deep breath and faced straight ahead. The quiet was positively eerie when she stepped down off that bus onto the dusty street. Except for the idle of the bus engine and the lonely bark of a dog somewhere in the distance, all was silent. Where was he? Would he come? The driver, at least, showed some concern.

"Ride's not here," he said, looking around them.

Cassie nodded nervously. "He knew I was coming."

"Sweetheart?"

The irony of it twisted her mouth into the semblance of a smile. He seemed to take that for some sort of confirmation.

"Well, he'll be along then. Meanwhile, you're safe as a babe in her crib."

She looked skeptical at that, but he merely chuckled.

"No, really. Why, there isn't a locked door in this town. Shoot, half the cars got keys in the ignitions. Now El Paso, that would be something else, but between here and there—and that's miles—there's nothing and nobody that would do you harm, not counting the rattlers, of course."

Rattlers? Cassie nervously glanced down at the ground around her feet.

"Not here!" the driver said, laughing and throwing out an arm. "Out yonder. You just don't go wandering off and you'll be fine." He hesitated a moment, then grabbed her hand and shook it. "So long now. Got a schedule to keep. Ride with us again sometime."

She had to put her hands behind her to keep from reaching out to pull him back as he climbed onto the big bus. She stood watching helplessly as the door closed with a *swoosh* and the bus pulled away. When even the grind of the engines had dwindled into silence, she slowly took stock around her. A single street lamp burned high on a pole above her, casting a weak halo of light upon the ground. The immediate area was virtually deserted. Several blocks over she could see the flashing neon sign of a small, dingy bar, but even it seemed strangely silent. In the distance, the headlights of a car flowed along the elevated ribbon of the highway and then was gone. Cassie stood alone in the stillness and the silence. Nothing had ever seemed so bleak. She had never felt so alone. She closed her eyes for a moment. Then she sat down on the bench and took out his letters again. They were all she had to give her hope, all she had to hold on to.

The sun was coming up by the time he reached Van Horn. Leon cursed himself fluently, saying the worst words in Spanish just as if his mother were riding beside him. Not that May Paradise remained ignorant of Spanish curse words after forty-four years lived in Texas west of the Pecos River. It was, as Leon might have explained if pressed, a sign of respect. No true gentleman cussed in front of his mother in her native tongue, even if she'd taught him the words herself, which May had not. That honor had gone to Leon's older brother, who had learned them from the hands on the Far Gone, the Presidio County ranch where Gerald and May Paradise had raised their three sons. Leon had dutifully passed on the Spanish *imprecaciónes* to his younger brother, Bo, now a senior at the university in Alpine. The three boys had gleefully stomped around the "big house" on the Far Gone, rattling off insults and filthy names. May had ignored them for the most part, but the first time one of them had blurted one of those words in front of a guest of Mexican descent, May had cuffed him smartly.

Leon wished somebody would cuff him now. How could he have been so stupid as to leave the *blankety-blank* radio receiver at home? He wagged that *blankety-blank* thing with him everywhere he went, but last night, of all times, he'd walked out and left it sitting on the *blankety-blank* couch, where he'd put it after repairing it earlier in the day so that he wouldn't forget it! Then, in the middle of nowhere, when the *blankety-blank* carburetor had broken down on his *blankety-blank* truck, he'd had no way to arrange for someone else to meet her. He wouldn't be surprised to find that she'd gotten on another bus and headed back to West Virginia. He almost hoped she had.

Truth be told, Leon had never been so torn about anything in his life. He wanted a wife, and he wasn't the first old boy in the county to take this particular route to find one. On the other hand, he figured this was the chanciest thing he'd ever done, and he was more than a little nervous about it. Why, oh, why, had he sent for her? Why hadn't he gotten to know her some better first, called her up on the phone at that country store where she'd worked, or something? Foolish, foolish, foolish. And the truck breaking down with him leaving that radio at home at the same time had to be some kind of ill omen. Lord, he'd stepped in it now, spent his hard-earned money for nothing, more than likely—or worse, for a hatful of headache. Why on earth had he done it?

He asked himself that silently and answered himself out loud in some choice Spanish words, but deep down he knew why. It was that little sketch that had gotten to him. Her letters had been compelling but oddly impersonal. He was always a little frustrated upon reading one, but they seemed to put him in mind of something important to say, something that he needed to get down on paper right quick like, so that he always found himself writing back immediately. Then that sketch had come. Done in plain pencil on an en-

velope smoothed flat with a hot iron, it was smudged from
rough handling in the mail, the boldest lines softened and
the delicate ones gently smudged, giving it a spooky kind
of aura that made it seem more real than any snapshot or
formal portrait. His heart had lurched at his first sight of
that feminine face with its almost pointy chin and high,
broad cheekbones, small but full mouth, turned-up nose,
big oval eyes slightly tilted upward at the outer edges beneath wispy, gently arched eyebrows somehow made a
dominant feature. It was the face of an angel, an other-
worldly creature not meant for the touch of mere mortal
man.

She was a myth, a figment of some artist's imagination.
The name signed in the corner—Newt—with simple yet
fanciful strokes seemed to confirm that notion, but the ac-
companying letter had said that he was her brother and that
no camera was able to provide a "truer" likeness. Pure curiosity had spurred Leon to write Dodie for a description.
What he'd received had been enough to truly fire his imagination. "Plenty of curves," Dodie had written, "especially on top. Just average height. Maybe five-five. Ash
blond hair cut straight just below the nape of her neck. No
curls. Heart-shaped face. Pretty. The Esterbridge eyes,
green as pine needles. Good teeth. Little hands and feet."
Dodie's no-nonsense, unadorned words had given his angel new dimension, a *womanly, human* dimension. Yet, he
couldn't quite put that face with the body his mind con-
jured.

He had dreamed of her, hot, erotic, lusty dreams. Then
he'd gotten that one letter in which she'd opened up a bit
about her late husband, and he'd decided she was worth
taking a chance on, a woman who knew what it meant to
love. That was the reason he had fired off that money order after receiving word that she was interested in coming
to Texas. Now he knew he was bound for disappointment.
She wasn't real, this woman in his head. Cassie couldn't fit
the image that his mind had fashioned. It would be easier

for both of them if she'd just given up or gotten mad and headed back to West Virginia. Lord, what would a West Virginia mountain girl do out here on this hot, dusty desert, anyway? Maybe she could handle not getting into town more than once or twice a month, but the forty-one miles of flat dirt road that lay between the ranch and Van Horn was enough to give even a hermit second thoughts. Hadn't his own brother told him that no cowboy in his right mind would take on a place like the Paradise? And while Dale might be bossy as a rooster in a hen house, he was a good cowboy, a damn fine cowboy. West of the Pecos there was no greater compliment.

Full of foreboding, Leon turned the pickup into the gasoline station at the corner of the state highway and Van Horn's main street and parked it in front of the pump. Pushing his hand through his wavy hair, he grabbed his hat—the good one, the silk lined, brown beaver with the tall Calgary crown and four-inch brim—and ducked out of the truck. He placed the hat on his head, adjusted it and walked briskly down the street toward the bus stop without giving his truck a second thought. The proprietor would be along any minute to open up. Recognizing Leon's truck, he'd fill it with gasoline, check the radiator and using the key left in the ignition, move it to one side to await Leon's eventual return, at which point they'd exchange greetings and news but, as it was not the end of the month, no money. Leon wasn't the only one to get such treatment, but he was one of the few. He had earned a reputation for being hardworking, fair dealing and prompt in paying. In fact, Leon was so well thought of that had one local merchant claimed to have been cheated by him, the rest would have called that one a liar—and stood back and watched while Leon cleaned the liar's clock.

Such thoughts were far from Leon's mind, however, as he crossed the street, arms swinging at his sides and boot heels clopping on the pavement. He leaped the steps up to the raised sidewalk and lengthened his strides, passing the café's picture windows. A glimmer of light in the shad-owed interior told him that Sofía had already begun her day and was heating up the grill. He thought longingly of a cup of hot coffee and a big breakfast, but before he could even consider giving in to temptation, he had turned the corner and stopped dead in his tracks.

She was lying on her side on the wooden bench, her head pillowed on a folded arm, knees drawn up, skirt tucked tightly around bare legs. She wore tan sandals and a short-sleeved dress with little blue and green flowers printed on it. Her straight, smoky blond hair fell over her forearm and onto the bench seat. She was shivering. And asleep.

For an instant, he considered turning around and walk-ing back the way he'd come. She was bound to be hurt and angry and emotional, and he couldn't blame her. He braced himself for the onslaught of female histrionics that was sure to come. Still, he was no coward, and it would be a dress-ing-down he well deserved. Besides, he was more than a little curious to see just exactly what she looked like. He had that sketch in mind, this angelic image, and in some ways he wanted it dispelled. He took a deep breath, walked forward on the balls of his feet and stood with his hands on his hips looking down at her. In profile, her face seemed childlike and innocent, angelic, even. But then his eyes raked over her body and the angel became a woman.

"Plenty of curves," Dodie had said, and Dodie was right. The way her dress was tucked around her left little to the imagination concerning her shape, especially where her hipbone curved down into the narrow valley of her waist and the lush swells of her breasts rose through the scooped neck of a well filled bodice. He looked at her tiny feet and the small hand that lay against the bench seat next to her gently rounded belly. No doubt about it. This was Cassie, and she was real, blood-and-bones female. It might be worth putting up with the pouting and acrimony, after all. He went down on his haunches, pushed his hat back and allowed himself another long look at her. The face might be angelic, but the body was made for sin, and that was just the direction in which his imagination was taking him.

Hold on now, buster, he told himself sternly. *Let's get to know the little gal first. One wrong step and you could find yourself hog-tied in matrimonial ropes, only to find out later you don't like anything about her but her looks. On the other hand, she might not like you or this setup. This just might be as close as you get.*

He cocked his head, reached out to touch her face, thought better of it and withdrew. But he was going to have to wake her sooner or later. He pushed his hat back, considering, then cleared his throat. Nothing. He reached for her shoulder to nudge her, spied the black grease in the creases of his knuckles and decided against touching her dress. He wouldn't want to do any irreparable damage. He gently stroked her arm below the edge of her sleeve. Invisible light seemed to radiate up his arm. He caught his breath as eyelids studded with glistening blond lashes slowly lifted, and eyes of a clear, mossy green pinned him.

"Oh," she said after a moment, struggling to sit up. One hand went to her skirt, and the other went to her hair. The skirt came down over her knees, and the hair swung into place, flowing from a center part as smoothly as silk. She blinked. "I'm sorry. I guess I fell asleep."

She was sorry. He was hours and hours late, and *she* was sorry. He looked away, feeling guilty as all get-out. A worried expression came into her eyes, and he quickly moved to dispel it, doffing his hat.

"Apologies all mine, ma'am. Truck broke down out in the middle of nowhere, and I didn't have a radio. All I could do was fix it. Actually, I forgot it, radio that is."

"Oh, I see. Well, then, it couldn't be helped, could it?" She smiled at him. Her teeth were white and straight, except for one on the bottom front that lapped slightly over its neighbor.

Leon noted that tiny imperfection with something akin to relief. She was not perfect, after all. Pretty close to it, though. But she was real. And here. And looking at him with a certain amount of puzzlement. He realized suddenly that he was staring. He lifted a hand and scratched the back of his neck, giving himself an excuse for the abrupt shift of his gaze.

"Um, you...you must've been awful tired," he muttered.

She nodded and looked down at her hands nervously. "Guess so. I never expected to go to sleep when I lay down here. It was so...." She shrugged. "Well, it was kind of spooky." She looked up quickly. "Strange place, you know. Nobody around."

He felt like a heel. "Listen, I'm sure sorry. There just wasn't anything I could do. The da—durn carburetor clogged up, so the engine conked, and I was halfway between the house and town, better'n twenty miles either way, with nary a human being in between, and like a ninny I left the radio receiver sitting on the couch where it did me a damn—*dang* lot of good."

She grinned at him. "So you just fixed it, huh?"

He spread his hands and dropped them to his knees. "Wasn't anything else to do."

Her grin broadened. "If it had been Pa or Newt or anybody else I ever knew except...." The grin faltered, but she hurried on. "Well, we'd all still be walking, for sure."

The implication registered, and he was flattered. "Oh. Well, I reckon I'm fairly handy with tools, but out here you have to be—even if you *remember* the dadblasted radio!"

She laughed, and he found himself feeling uncommonly clever.

"I couldn't have gotten here any sooner," he went on, "but I could've called somebody to come for you, instead of leaving you out here all by your lonesome."

She shook her head, hunching her shoulders. "It's okay. I guess I wasn't as scared as I thought. I seemed to have gone right off to sleep." She rubbed her hands briskly over her arms, and he realized that she was bound to be chilly even though the sun was practically up. He rose to his full height.

"Let's get you in off the sidewalk and have us a bite of breakfast. Okay?"

She beamed at him. "Great! I'm hungry, all right."

He beamed back, feeling a little ridiculous and a lot awkward but wanting very much to put her at her ease. "Know what you mean. My belly thinks my throat's been cut."

She laughed a bit too heartily at that and stood, only to sway uncertainly back toward the bench.

"Whoa!" His hands shot out and grabbed her around the waist. She felt warmly solid, and heat rushed instantly to his groin. He actually thought of kissing her, and if that wasn't rushing things he didn't know what was. He grabbed his hands back again, not knowing whether her shocked look was from his manhandling or from having nearly fallen. He swallowed a sudden lump in his throat and peered into her eyes, trying to judge her condition without confronting any embarrassing emotions. "You steady now?"

She licked her lips, and he wished mightily that she hadn't. "Yes. Steady. Thanks."

He nodded and pulled his hat forward, breathing harder than was reasonable. "Here we go, then." He held out an arm, his hand hovering at her back.

She turned with him, then abruptly turned back. "My things!" She indicated the bench.

He cocked his head, spying for the first time the battered brown vinyl suitcase and small cardboard box that were under the bench. Not much to travel cross-country with. Maybe she wasn't planning to stay long. He frowned, pushing away the thought. "They'll be fine here for the time being," he told her. "Won't nobody bother them. I'll carry them over to the truck later."

She seemed to accept this without question and turned to walk beside him around the corner to the door of the café.

They were the first customers of the day, and he had to beat on the door to get Sofía to open up. She came running from the kitchen, her rotund body bouncing in several directions. "Leon!" she exclaimed in greeting, giving his name an exotic Spanish pronunciation. She threw open her arms in welcome even as her dark eyes flashed over his companion. "Who have you got there, eh?" Without waiting for his answer, she offered her plump hand to Cassie and said in a voice heavily influenced by her native Spanish, "I am Sofía. It's nice to meet you."

Cassie put her small hand in Sofía's. "I'm Cassie, ma'am, Cassie Hunter, from West Virginia."

Sofía looked at Leon in surprise. "Oh, she gots an accent!"

Cassie's expressive eyebrows rose slightly. Leon chuckled. "Doesn't everybody?" he said.

"You don't!" Sofía exclaimed.

"That's not what you used to say," he laughingly reminded her, exaggerating his drawl on every syllable.

She let go of Cassie's hand and propped her fists against the squarish mounds of her hips. "That was before my English got good!" she declared.

Leon slid an amused look at Cassie. "She said, that was before her English got good," he translated needlessly.

Cassie's green eyes sparkled. Muttering in Spanish, Sofía swatted playfully at his head, and he pretended to swerve out of the way, grinning. Sofía turned, very much on her dignity. "Just for that," she said over her shoulder, "you can pour your own coffee."

"What?" he called after her. "You gonna pass up a chance to pour coffee in my lap?"

Sofía stuck her nose in the air and waddled into the kitchen. Leon laughed, and with a hand at her elbow, escorted Cassie to a booth in the corner, hanging his hat on the hat tree as he passed it.

"Did she really do that?" Cassie asked.

"Pour coffee in my lap? Yes, ma'am. It was my fault, though. She was standing at my shoulder with the pot and I was holding the cup up, but I was talking to a fellow and sort of forgot what I was doing. I set the cup down just as she started to pour."

Cassie lifted a hand to her mouth, obviously moved by sympathy. "Oh, my goodness!"

He cocked his head, feeling wicked and a little giddy. "You ever seen a cowboy strip down to his skivvies in public?"

The hand dropped. "You didn't," she said, looking scandalized.

He nudged her into the booth, leaning forward as she sank down. He braced one hand on the back of the booth and the other on the edge of the table. "Ma'am, you never saw a fellow move so fast."

Her eyes grew very large and filled with empathy. "Well, I guess you didn't have much choice, did you?"

He shook his head. "Wouldn't have been so bad, really, but about the time I peeled 'em down, the fellow I was talking to threw a glass of ice water at me."

She saw the lie in his eyes and started to laugh. "Oh, you! You're making that up."

He grinned. "Actually, he threw the water before I got my belt unbuckled, and that cooled me right off. But, man, did I ever take a ribbing, walking around in wet jeans!"

"And you haven't let poor Sofía forget it, have you?"

He shook his head, laughing. "Want a cup? I promise not to pour it in your lap."

She wrinkled her nose and slid her gaze away. "Actually, I never learned to drink it."

He knew he should straighten up, put some distance between them now that the joke was over, but he didn't. "Want something else, then?"

She looked at him sheepishly. "Soda pop?"

He chuckled. "Sure. Okay." Again he postponed pulling back, naming a popular brand of cola.

She nodded, whispering, "Fine. Thank you."

He pushed back as far as possible without taking his hands from the table. "Sofía makes a great rancher's breakfast. Hash browns, bacon, omelet."

"Sounds good, but I don't think I could eat that much."

"Just the omelet, then? Or maybe you'd like something else?" He was making her uncomfortable, and he didn't want to make her uncomfortable. He wanted to make her think about what he was thinking about, and it was too soon for that, much too soon. He clamped down and straightened up. "I'll get us a menu."

She turned her head sharply and for an instant seemed to be reaching out, but then her hand veered toward her hair and smoothed it—not that it needed smoothing. It was as sleek and shiny as satin. He curled his hands into fists to keep from touching it.

"The omelet will do fine," she told him, smiling shyly.

He nodded, not trusting himself to speak, and backed away. Oh, man. This wasn't going to do at all. She was a powerful package of woman, and he was already on the verge of doing something remarkably stupid. She had come out here to meet him and, ostensibly, investigate the possibility of marriage. Whether or not that investigation would get as far as the bedroom remained to be seen, and he was bound to scare her off—or worse yet, wind up unhappily hitched—if he let his hormones run away with him.

He was going to have to cool off before he made a mess of things, keep her at a distance somehow, and that wasn't going to be easy with the two of them bumping around his little house. On the other hand, how was he supposed to get to know this woman if he didn't take her out to the Paradise with him? And why hadn't he thought of this before?

He hurried away to wash his hands, deliver their order to Sofía and fetch coffee and soda. He had a problem, and he had to find a solution, fast.

Chapter Two

Cassie cut through the layers of cheese, chili and onions to the omelet below, herded a chunk of it onto her fork, and lifted it to her mouth with as much nonchalance as she could manage. She smiled at Leon Paradise and began to chew, biting into a sizable piece of jalapeño pepper. Fire squirted into her mouth and bathed her throat. She coughed as discreetly as possible, her eyes tearing and her mouth full of egg, cheese, chili, onions and pepper. Leon's fork froze in midair, and he lifted concerned eyes to her.

"Something wrong?"

She shook her head, offered a weak smile and quickly swallowed. "Fine!" she squeaked, tears rolling down her cheeks.

He put his fork down and pushed her soft-drink glass closer to her hand. "Little too spicy, is it? I should've warned you. Actually, I should've warned Sofía to go easy. You West Virginians probably aren't used to eating fire like us West Texans. Just didn't think. Sorry."

She gulped cola while he talked, then gasped cool air. "It's good," she croaked. "Hot but good."

"Let me get you something else," he said, but she didn't want him to think she was going to need coddling.

Lord knew she'd made a bad enough impression already, sleeping on a public bench like some hobo! Now here she sat in a dress she'd worn three days, her face and body unwashed and her hair uncombed. Her last chance to clean up and make herself presentable had been in the ladies' room of the last restaurant at which the bus had stopped, and that seemed like ages ago now. He slid toward the edge of the booth, and she made a grab for his wrist. He looked startled for a moment, then suddenly relaxed. She cleared her throat. "Really, I like it."

He looked down at her hand curled over his wrist and back up again. He had the nicest eyes, a soft, buttery brown without the slightest hint of red, like a new fawn. His lashes were a darker brown, thick and long, as pretty as any girl's, and there were crinkles at the outside corners of his eyes, as if he smiled a lot. The straight slashes of his eyebrows were darker still, but his hair was a light golden brown streaked with pale yellow. A little too long, it flowed back from his temples in waves and splayed around his shirt collar. A single lock fell forward from a little swirl above his left eye. She figured that if it was cut short enough, it would stick up there in a cowlick.

She could imagine him as a little boy with his hair sticking up in front and freckles splattered across cheeks still round and a nose not yet strong and without that tiny hump just at the bridge. He must have been a cute boy because he was a good-looking man, not handsome really, for his features were a bit too sharp and angular, but strongly male, despite the eyes, and very, very striking. He could look awfully severe when he frowned, but he could make her heart flutter, too. He was doing that now. She swallowed and licked her lips, suddenly feeling parched again. He closed his eyes, then opened them and gently removed himself from her touch. She felt as if he'd slapped her. Didn't he like to be touched? Maybe he just didn't like to be touched by her. That was a depressing thought, not just because she so desperately needed him to like her but because she so much liked him.

He reached for a steaming tortilla, buttered it, rolled it and pushed it into her hand. "Eat that," he said. "It'll take the bite out some."

It didn't look particularly appetizing. A flat, white, round thing with brown spots. But she bit off the end and found it quite tasty, though subtly flavored. "This is good," she said. "What's in it?"

He shrugged. "Flour, lard, a little water, I imagine. Nothing much."

"Tastes pretty good for nothing much."

"That's the way folks out here cook. Use a few ingredients a lot of ways. Mexican influence, I suppose."

"Sounds pretty self-sufficient," she commented, digging into her omelet again and carefully pushing aside a chunk of pepper.

He scooted over and picked up his own fork. "That's pretty much what you've got to be out here," he said, "self-sufficient. Otherwise, you're going to find yourself in a whole lot of trouble sooner or later."

Cassie savored her food for a moment, then swallowed. It was still spicy, but without the pepper it didn't scorch the hide off the inside of her mouth. She'd never had chili for breakfast before, but she supposed she could get used to it. That decided, she plunged into the omelet and turned her mind back to the conversation. "What kind of trouble?"

He crumbled his bacon over the top of his chili and started in again. "Bad trouble. Heatstroke, starvation, thirst, broken bones, snakebites, exposure."

She put her fork down. "Sounds downright dangerous."

He inclined his head. "Yes, ma'am. Those of us who live out on the range are miles and miles away from medical attention of any kind, and this is a tough land. 'Course, we got better communication now, shortwave and CB radios, cellular dish telephones. That's good, but you're still pretty much on your own out there, especially on horseback. Wheels aren't no guarantee, either, though.

"Had a fellow over northeast of here hunting up cattle in the Delaware range. Drove his truck up a fair slope onto what he thought was a rock shelf. Shelf was sand. It gave way beneath his outside tires. Truck rolled down the slope and slid into a ravine. Broke him up pretty bad, legs, ribs, collarbone, jaw. He got on the radio and finally made contact. We gathered up and went out looking. Took us sixteen hours to find that ravine."

Cassie leaned forward, her own food forgotten. "What happened?"

He swallowed and grabbed a tortilla. "We poured whiskey down him, got him good and drunk. Soon as he passed out, we hauled him out of there, bedded him down in the back of a truck and hauled *nalgas* into El Paso to the hospital."

"El Paso! Why, that's—"

"A hundred and fifteen miles from this very spot," he said.

Her mouth fell open. "Isn't there anything closer?"

He shook his head, waving his fork around. "Oh, we've got a sawbones, and he's pretty good, too, but we haven't got the facilities for the serious stuff."

Two and a half hours! she thought, but then she reminded herself that thirty miles on foot was nearly impossible, and that was how far she'd have to go and her only way to get to decent medical care back home in West Virginia. Still, she wondered what she'd gotten herself into. But no matter. She was here now, and she couldn't go back. She'd just have to make the best of it, and she sensed that the best of it was Leon Paradise himself.

She hoped he liked her as much as she liked him so far. He seemed a real capable man, but then he'd have to be if what he said about living out here was true, and she didn't doubt it. Leon Paradise was not the sort of man a person doubted. She felt a deep satisfaction in having judged him so well. She was safe with this man. He was not only capable but generous and clever, too. More than that, he was good company, and under the circumstances, she couldn't ask for much more. If only he liked her well enough to keep her—and the boys. Feeling a pang in the vicinity of her heart, she pushed thoughts of the boys away and concentrated on eating her omelet, careful to pick out as much of the hot stuff as possible.

Ten minutes later, Leon pushed away his plate, refilled his coffee cup and settled back to study her. She felt his gaze moving over her face and upper body but kept her eyes averted, determined not to show her discomfort. When she'd drained the last drop from her soda glass, he put his coffee cup down and leaned forward.

"We've got to make some decisions," he said gently.

She looked up. "Decisions?"

He looked down at the fingertip he was running around the edge of his cup. "I'm not sure what you expected, coming out here like this. Heck, I'm not sure what I expected. Well, no, now that's the thing, I suppose. What I *don't* expect, that is."

He lifted his gaze to hers. She didn't try to hide her confusion. He shook his head and looked back down at the cup. "What I mean is, I wouldn't want you to think I expect more than...us getting to know each other and..." He cleared his throat and shifted in his seat, then said abruptly, "I've got some friends you can stay with, Wendell and Nadine Mott. They're quite a bit older, but I'm sure they won't mind having you. Nadine was saying just the other day how much they miss their daughter since she got grown and moved off. Y'all will do fine together."

Cassie's heart sank like a stone. He didn't like her. She wasn't what he was looking for. He was disappointed. She put her head to her hand, elbow on the table, and tried to think. She could change, she just needed a chance to figure out what he wanted, to make herself useful. "I thought I'd be staying with you," she said softly.

His head jerked up. He opened his mouth, then closed it. His hand came up and he rubbed behind his ear. "Well, my place is pretty isolated," he said, "and small."

She shrugged. "I don't mind. I'm used to small houses and such."

He rubbed his throat. "It'd be just the two of us, and me, I'm working all day. You'd probably get lonely."

"I could help out," she said. "I'm strong, and I'm used to hard work. Why, back home, we do our laundry on a scrub board in a tub out behind the house, and we chop our own wood, and—"

He lifted a hand to silence her. "I—I wouldn't expect none of that. You're not out here for working. You're here as a . . . a guest."

"But I'm not!" she argued. "I didn't come all this way to see how I'd work out as *company*. I came to see how I'd work out as . . . as a *partner*." She felt herself blushing, but she didn't drop her gaze. Neither did he, but he lifted a hand to the back of his neck, rubbing there.

"I've got two bedrooms," he said. "You could stay in one until. . .I mean, that is, if. . ." His hand moved to stroke his jaw. "The house isn't much, now," he stumbled on. "It's an old house. Needs paint and adding on—I've been meaning to do that—but it's a sturdy house, and it's got a real floor in it, electricity and all. No hot water, but it just needs buying a tank and putting it in. I been meaning to do that, too. Still and all, you're welcome, but I'm just warning you, it could be a shade lonesome." He seemed struck by a thought, narrowed his eyes and leaned forward on one elbow. "You don't by chance ride a horse, do you, 'cause you could come along then just for the ride."

She bit her lip. "No. But I'm not scared of them, either, and I'd surely love to learn!"

He rubbed a hand over his face. "Well, as to that, I'll see you do, but right now I better ride the range alone." He looked at her levelly. "It's not that I couldn't use the company or the help, it's just that I wouldn't want nothing to happen to you."

She was disappointed, but what could she say? She hunched her shoulders and nodded. "All right, Leon, if you say so."

"You sure you won't mind the days alone?" he asked.

She thought of her son and brothers, but forced a smile. "I won't mind."

"I hope not," he said softly. Then he grimaced and laid his hands flat on the tabletop. "Look, Cassie, I don't know what's going to happen with us, and neither do you. No one does. But I'll say this, you're a sight more promising than any other female I've come across, and I won't lie to you. I've not ever been nobody's angel, but... Well, it's been a long time." He looked into her eyes. His had gone all soft and glowing. "It's been a long time," he repeated, "but I'm hopeful, and I thank you for that much, anyway."

She smiled, feeling desperate, hopeful and lucky. And lower than a skunk. She knew she ought to tell him about Petey and her brothers. She knew she ought to say right out how she had nowhere else to go and no one else to go to, but the danger that he'd draw back was too great yet, and she'd promised the boys she'd send for them, all six of them. So she bit back the need to speak and said a silent prayer. *Let it work. Oh, let it work out between us. Please, Lord, let it work.*

"Truth is," Leon said softly, "I hadn't planned on leaving you with the Motts. They don't even know about you. I figured that'd be best until we see which way this thing is going for sure. It's just that... well, now that I've..." He lifted his eyebrows, took a deep breath, and plunged on. "You're a mighty powerful temptation, Cassie, and I don't want to do anything to... ruin our chances."

Relief swept through her and the kind of heat she hadn't felt since... She didn't want to think about Jos. She didn't want to think at all. She had hope, real hope, for the first time in years, and in that moment she knew that she wasn't going to tell Leon anything that might "ruin their chances." She reached across the table and took his hand.

"Can we go now?"

His hand tightened on hers, and a slow smile spread across his face. "I'll just get the check."

It was the most magnificent land she'd ever seen. Mountains stood on every side, but not the great, forested, deep valley mountains of home. These ranges were tough, rocky, tumbledown piles separated by broad, flat, sandy valleys studded by a variety of cacti and grasses, purple sage and a plant that Leon called *ocotillo,* which looked like a bunch of prickly, greenish soda straws clumped together. Not a tree was in sight, not a vine, not a fern, not an ivy but, oh, what an abundance of blue sky and wide-open spaces! It made a person feel tiny and humble. It made a person feel free.

During the drive to the ranch, Leon played cassettes and talked some. The cowboy music wasn't a lot different in style from the mountain music native to West Virginia, but it varied greatly in substance. She would not have guessed that modern cowboys were so concerned with romance and broken hearts, or rodeos and nightclubs. There were no paeans to humble log cabins or the mountains of home, no rousing celebrations of life even at its most mean, no sad melodies bemoaning the ultimate tragedy of death, no lyrical ditties extolling the beauty of nature, no angry ballads decrying the world's many injustices. There were lots of toe-tapping dance tunes and suggestive lyrics. Most surprising of all, however, was that Leon seemed to know every one by heart and as often as not sang along. He had a fair voice and absolutely no embarrassment about using it. Every so often, she'd ask a question about the country-

side or the ranch. He'd answer, then come back with a
question of his own about her home or her trip out West.
Mostly, though, he sang with the music and she watched the
landscape.

It was warm, and the truck had an air conditioner, but he
didn't offer to turn it on and she didn't ask him to. As long
as they were moving with the windows rolled down, she was
comfortable. And move they did, at amazing speeds. The
only time he slowed was to turn a corner, and only two of
those lay between Van Horn and the ranch. The second one
led them onto a dirt road. Dust billowed behind them, but
still the windows stayed down and the air conditioner stayed
off.

Nearly an hour after leaving Van Horn, they swung
around the end of a mountain chain and headed for a jum-
ble of buildings and fences in the distance. Cassie sat up
straight in her seat. Leon quit singing and nodded toward
the compound.

"That's it. That's the Paradise."

"It begins here?" Cassie asked.

He chuckled and shook his head. "No, ma'am. It began
at that last fence back there."

She widened her eyes. "All the way back *that* far?"

"And on about the same distance from here in two more
directions," he said, pointing forward and to the right.

Cassie's mouth fell open. "Good Lord above!"

He propped an elbow in the window and grinned.
"That's how I feel about it, too. Sometimes I look out over
all this and I wonder if it's a joke, if somebody in a suit is
going to come along and say, 'Pack it up, Leon, and pitch
you a tent in town. Nobody's allowed to own this much of
the earth.' Others own more, mind you, but by God this
chunk of it's mine, and I'd fight every suit in the world to
keep it."

"Gracious," she said, "I've never even owned my own
cabin, but if I did, I'd be just like you about it."

"Of like minds," he said, smiling.

She smiled, too. Such a place had to have room for six boys, didn't it? She just knew they'd love it out here, and that would give them something in common with Leon.

She listened as he pointed out the various structures. There was the homeplace gate first, two impressive stair-stepped sections with the name of the ranch, spelled out in iron letters a foot tall and flanked by gigantic replicas of the Paradise brand, a letter P against a mountain peak. Beyond this was a large, empty corral built of metal pipe, then two smaller ones flanking a big, pale blue, metal barn. A horse stood in the corner of one corral, munching hay from a feeder fashioned from half a metal barrel. A windmill pumped a trickle of water into a pair of low, round, metal troughs inside the corrals. Another taller windmill with a large cylindrical tank and a jointed flue elevated between its legs stood beside a small, square, stuccoed structure that could only be the house. The slightly pitched roof was made of split-wood shingles weathered the same silvery gray as the flat-roofed porch. A stovepipe poked up through one end, and a satellite dish, which Leon explained was for the telephone, perched on the other. The walls were more tan than white as time and blowing sand had blasted the paint from the adobe. The glass in the few windows was bare, grimy and pitted, the paint around their wooden frames, peeling. The yard was sand, sand and nothing else. It was clear where Leon's priorities lay. The barn, corrals, windmills and tank looked spanking new. The house, even with the satellite dish, looked as if it had been abandoned in a previous century.

Leon pulled the pickup to a stop about five feet from the porch, hopped out and lifted her suitcase and box from the truck bed. Cassie let herself out on her side while he loped around the end of the vehicle and up onto the porch. He shouldered the door open and disappeared inside the house. Cassie followed slowly, feeling the heat more now and shading her eyes from the sun with her hands as she continued to look around. Wooden planks had been laid out around and below the big windmill. She found that curious but not nearly as curious as the house.

She stepped up into the shade of the porch, cringing inwardly at the scrape of her sandals on the wood. Every sound seemed magnified out here in the midst of so much silence. She could almost hear the wind, it was that quiet. She could hear, too, Leon clumping around inside the house. She passed through the open door, noting with satisfaction the thickness of the walls, and into the shadowy interior. Leon appeared through a curtained doorway across the room.

"I put your stuff in there." He motioned to the room behind him, then stepped sideways and indicated another doorway in the same wall. "Kitchen's in there. Bathroom's off the back of it." He pointed to a curtained door in a perpendicular wall. "That's my room. It opens into the kitchen, too. That's all there is. Make yourself to home."

"Thanks." Cassie walked around peeking into the various rooms, then took in the one in which she stood. It was maybe twelve or thirteen feet square. The walls were a dirty white and bisected with black electrical wires ending in exposed outlet boxes. An oval braided rug in shades of brown covered most of the white brick floor. The couch, which still held the forgotten radio receiver, was orange vinyl with wooden arms and legs, the old-fashioned kind with a back that laid down level with the seat to form a rough bed. The chair, a low rocker, matched the couch in style if not in color. Its drab green upholstery was covered with an old quilt that looked far more comfortable than the tweedy cushions. Two empty nail kegs served as side tables, one beside the rocker, one beside the couch. The only lamp in the room, yellow-painted metal with a globe and metal shade, stood at one end of the couch. Magazines were stacked next to it. Their spines identified them all as having to do with cattle or horse breeding.

The wall against which the porch was built was covered with shelves from the edge of the door to the corner. They contained a number of books, many of them paperbacks, a small stereo system with a radio and a tape deck, and an impressive collection of tapes. There were also several wood carvings and a few pieces of rusty barbed wire mounted on stained plaques. The room offered no windows except the one in the front door, but she had glimpsed one in the outside wall of Leon's room and another in her own. Two old branding irons were crisscrossed and mounted on the wall above the sofa, the only effort, apparently, at decoration. It was a room that fairly screamed for a woman's touch. She was already picturing the walls and wires painted a soft buttery yellow and stenciled with ivy—well, maybe cactus—and the furniture draped in soft blue blankets scattered with little orange pillows needlepointed with...Indian designs, stick figures or something. Newt could help there. The rugs should be—

Leon cleared his throat and leaned against the wall, arms folded across his chest. ''Well?''

She pushed the decorating ideas aside and presented him with a pleasant face. ''It's not much smaller than Pa's house,'' she said, ''and a mite larger than the one Jos and I had. It's a whole lot sturdier than either, though. Adobe, isn't it?''

''Yes, ma'am. Not this new, prefab stuff, either. Fellow I bought it from said it was built back in the Twenties. Floors, kitchen and bath were added later, and I put the electric generator in myself. I crank it up in the evenings when I want to listen to the stereo or read or...well, there isn't much else to do,'' he admitted sheepishly, one hand smoothing the back of his neck.

''It sounds fine,'' she declared with a nod. ''It sounds just fine. To tell you the truth, I'd just as soon sleep evenings, *this* evening, anyway.''

''Oh, hey, you must be dead on your feet,'' he said. ''Tell you what, I've got some work to do, so you might as well lay down for a while. There's food in the cold cellar beneath the kitchen floor, if you get hungry.''

"Would it be too much trouble if I had a bath first?" she asked hopefully.

Launching into action, he apologized profusely for the lack of hot water, assured her it would not be too cold, and showed her where she could find clean towels. There was a washer on the back porch, he told her, if she wanted to launder her things. She could do so by hand, she assured him. He told her to hang them on the line out back and they'd be dry within the hour, thanks to the desert climate. While she was putting her things away and selecting a clean change of clothing, Leon quickly traded his town clothes for work clothes: faded jeans, once black boots, a long-sleeved chambray shirt worn almost white, and a battered straw hat. He'd be back in plenty of time to make dinner, he told her, stubbornly refusing her offer to perform that chore.

"Later on," he assured her, "when you've had some rest and settled in." He stuffed a pair of slick-worn suede leather gloves into a hip pocket, turned up his collar, and went out, leaving her to soak away the road dirt.

The bathroom had clearly been added on, probably fifty years earlier. The walls were stuccoed in a different texture than the rest of the house, and the floors, ceiling and cabinets were wood. The sink was free-standing, and the bathtub was an old ivory claw-foot type with chipped enamel. The toilet had a painted wooden seat and a tank with a pull chain fastened to the wall above it.

She laid a change of clothing on the toilet lid, took a towel and a washcloth from the stacks inside one of the cabinets, pushed the rubber stopper into the drain and turned on the tap. At first, the water looked a little rusty but it soon ran clear. She closed the door, shrugged over its lack of a lock and disrobed. She felt safe enough. Leon wasn't even in the house, and even if he had been, she didn't think he'd walk in on her. Carrying a small bottle of baby shampoo from home and a bar of soap from the sink tray, she gingerly stepped over the side of the tub. The water was cold but not frigid. She knew that on a cooler day she'd be shivering, but for now it was bearable. Carefully, she slid down into the water, gave herself a moment to get used to it, then lay back to dunk her head. She shampooed, rinsed beneath the tap, then soaped up and eased back to soak the dirt away. The water was beginning to feel warmer as she grew used to it. She laid her head back on the rolled rim of the tub and closed her eyes.

He woke her hours later, knocking on the door and calling her name. "Cassie, are you in there?"

She sat up with a start, sloshing water, and her skin immediately prickled with gooseflesh. "Yes, I . . . What time is it?" She reached for a towel.

He chuckled and told her, his voice muffled by the door. It was the middle of the afternoon! "Get out of there before you dissolve."

She wrapped the towel around herself and looked down. Her hands and feet were wrinkled. Her hair was dry, she could tell, and she hadn't even combed it! "I—I'll be right out. I fell asleep."

She could hear the laughter in his voice. "You seem to have a habit of doing that."

She quickly toweled off and started to dress, pulling on panties and bra, jeans and T-shirt. "It's just the trip," she said. "Guess I was more tired than I thought."

"If you're decent now, you could hand me a towel," he said.

"A towel?" She took one from the cabinet and opened the door into the little nook off the kitchen. He had changed clothes again, this time into soft clean jeans with no belt and a white shirt with Western styling. He was wearing tan boots. His hair was wet and had sprinkled his shoulders with droplets of water.

He smiled. "I showered off under the windmill. Usually do. It cools you off real fast, and there's no danger of going to sleep that way, though I've seen the time I could sleep standing up, and that's no lie."

She had a sudden vision of him standing naked beneath that flue, and it must have shown on her face for he suddenly quirked one eyebrow and cocked his head. She felt heat flush her cheeks, and tried to cover the reaction by plucking at her hair. "It dried before I could comb it. I'll have to wet it again."

His gaze roamed over her. "You've got real pretty hair," he said softly, "even all tangled up like that."

She was shocked. "You think so?"

"Don't you?"

She didn't, actually. "It's just plain hair," she mumbled, "Nothing special."

He reached up and fingered a strand of it. "No, it's not. It's like silk, all shiny and soft." He looked into her eyes, and suddenly her heart was pounding and her mouth had gone dry. She gulped and licked her lips. He reeled back a step, hand going to his chest as if she'd punched him. "Good heavens, woman!" he exclaimed, his gaze on her mouth, and then he reached for her.

She dropped the towel, and her hands came up in surprise, but she knew what was happening and she welcomed it. He pulled her against him, and his arms slid around her. She turned her face up, and his head came down, his mouth claiming hers, fiercely at first and then with growing tenderness until it became a thing of such sweetness and joy that she felt tears gathering behind her lowered lids. He loosened his hold somewhat, one hand going to the small of her back, the other splaying between her shoulder blades. She went up on tiptoe and wrapped her arms around his shoulders. He smiled against her mouth, and his hands came up to frame her face as his lips lingered upon hers. He was not Jos, and it was not the same—and yet somehow it was. Somehow it was as loving and caring and sweet as ever it had been. He pulled back and looked at her. She didn't offer any explanation for the tears glistening in her eyes, and he didn't seem to require one. This time, his hands slid into her hair and he tilted her head just so, and when he kissed her, he slid his tongue into her mouth, and sweetness became heat that spread slowly throughout her body until she felt that she was melting from the inside out.

Awakened needs and desires gradually pushed out every thought, even awareness, until nothing existed but Leon and the fire he built inside her. Thoughts of Jos vanished. Comparisons were forgotten. Even the tangles in her hair ceased to exist. It was as if her nerve endings were super-charged, as if every sensation was magnified. He walked her backward a few steps and pressed her against the wall, pinning her there with his hips and plying her mouth with extreme dedication. She was caught in a heady swirl of sensual reciprocation, her breasts swelling and tightening, her mouth sucking and flexing, her tongue stroking and curling against his. Her body was clamoring for invasion and turning to liquid where he pressed against her. She wound her arms around his neck and hung on.

After a long while, with need twisting into frustration, she pulled her mouth from his and laid her head back against the wall. She needed to clear her mind and cool the fires. He put his forehead to hers and ran his thumbs down her throat to the indentation at its base. She knew what he felt there, the wild pulse of her blood. She closed her eyes, unwilling to allow embarrassment or shame or doubt to steal one moment of pleasure from her. He brushed his mouth over hers and sighed deeply. There were elements of contentment as well as frustration in that sigh. She felt her mouth curve into a poignant smile. He slid his hand around to the nape of her neck and pulled her head to his shoulder, his arm sliding around her in a tender embrace.

"Maybe I'm not crazy, after all," he whispered. Before she could ask what he meant by that, the shrill sound of a telephone sounded, startling her so that she jumped. He calmed her with a soothing caress. "The phone," he said, then reluctantly, he moved away from her. "Come on." He caught her hand and pulled her along behind him into the kitchen.

The phone was attached to the wall between the wood-topped brick counter and a painted cabinet. Leon picked up the receiver with his free hand and lifted it to his ear.

"Hello."

He grinned at nothing in particular, then slid that grin over to Cassie.

"Hello, Mom."

Cassie's eyebrows rose slightly as he turned and leaned a hip against the counter, keeping her hand in his.

"I went into town. Sorry I missed your call. Yeah, I know it's the middle of the week. No, nothing wrong."

He lifted Cassie's hand and brushed his lips across her knuckles. Then, looking into her eyes, he adjusted the telephone receiver and gently told his mother, "I've met a woman."

His eyes crinkled up at the corners as he smiled. "Yeah," he said, "I think it's about time, too."

Cassie pulled her hand away and ambled around the room, trying not to listen. She wasn't very successful.

"Maybe," he said. "Guess we'll see. No, no one you know."

She opened the oven door and peeked inside. It was clean and cold in a way that made her wonder idly if he'd ever used it.

"Uh-huh," he said, "she's *very* pretty, actually."

Caught off guard, she whirled around. His eyes met hers, then moved easily down her frame before coming back to her face. She felt her cheeks grow pink. He grinned and released her, dropping his gaze to the floor. She stood transfixed for several moments, vaguely aware that he mumbled something about not telling Dale, then she realized that the conversation had moved on to other subjects and she turned away as calmly as she could. *Very pretty.* She smiled to herself, nursing the first real sense of well-being that she'd felt in a very long, long time.

Chapter Three

It was so easy. Neither of them had expected it to be so easy. She was a mountain girl, from the cool, green slopes and peaks of West Virginia, whose life, home and heart had always been crowded with family and friends. He was a Texas cowboy, with roots sunk deep in twenty thousand acres of dry range desert, used to his own company and that of a few testy Bremer and longhorn crossbred cattle. Married at sixteen, widowed at nineteen, she had never even completed high school. He'd earned a college degree in animal husbandry. She constantly hummed the ageless tunes of her people, eschewing modern music as Jos and her sainted mother had done, but Leon was country through and through, and known to break into song whenever the mood struck, which seemed often since Cassie had arrived.

Leon was the first to admit that he wasn't getting as much work done as he ought, yet he left every morning by dawn, his belly full of breakfast cooked by an insistent Cassie and carrying a lunch she'd packed for him. The food wasn't what he was used to, a little bland for his taste, but that didn't matter. Neither did the fact that she'd practically taken over his house, rearranging things to suit herself and organizing cupboards. She'd even made an itemized list of the foodstuffs in the kitchen and the provisions he kept in the cold cellar. He didn't suppose she had much else to do while he was gone, and truthfully he didn't much care if she wrapped the place in gauze and tied it up with pink bows, as long as she was there and contented when he came in.

Every day he worked like a madman until early or mid afternoon, and headed home to stand beneath the windmill shower in the heat of the day—in his jeans, to spare Cassie any embarrassment and himself as much temptation as possible. He often wondered what she'd do if she walked outside and found him standing nude beneath the flue. It could have happened easily enough. Almost from the beginning, she'd been meeting him on the porch with clean clothing and a towel. But then she would go inside and shut the door, and he'd peel off his wet jeans, towel dry and quickly dress, wondering if she was as tempted to peek at him as he would have been to peek at her.

He always got a kick out of the shirts she chose for him to wear. The jeans were a given, as he owned nothing else, but some of the shirts that she picked out he'd had so long that he'd forgotten about them. Once she'd chosen a T-shirt that he had received as a gift years before but had *never* worn. The two-inch-wide green and orange vertical stripes just didn't appeal. Fortunately, the shirt was too small; he was glad to see that he had developed some muscular upper body weight since his reed-thin college days, and he had suggested half jokingly that they should throw the shirt away. She had scolded him for such waste, helped him wrestle the thing off and said she'd put it aside for someone else. Then she had shyly touched his chest, just barely dragging her fingertips across his bare skin before turning away, the shirt clutched to her breast. He had felt strong as a bull and just as randy, but they had talked about it and decided they were going to be sensible. They knew they had chemistry. No doubt about that. So now they would just see whether or not they were compatible. If not, no one would be hurt. If so...

If so was killing him. *Sensible* was killing him. But he was too happy to have her there to push it. He had never met a woman so easy to be around, so agreeable, so sweet, so *sexy*. Man, it was eating him alive! He couldn't keep his hands off of her, whether it was to slip his arms around her waist while she stood at the sink doing dishes or to hand her up into the saddle during their early-evening riding lessons. When they sat on the couch side by side, he couldn't help draping his arm loosely across her shoulders, and when they parted for the night, each headed for a different bedroom, he couldn't deny himself a good-night kiss even though he knew he couldn't let it get past just that. Then he'd lie awake for hours, wishing she'd come to him or talking himself out of going to her.

Perversely, he even designed activities so that he could touch her. He brought out his guitar and played for her, then offered to teach her some chords. He managed to get her sitting between his legs, his chest to her back, his arms bracketing hers as his hands coaxed her fingers into the correct positions. Once the generator was turned on of an evening, he'd slip a tape into the stereo deck and proceed to teach her the time-honored cowboy steps to western dancing. They had to go out onto the porch for room to dance, listening to the music through the open door, but she didn't seem to mind. She was a quick study, and often said that many of the steps were similar to dances she'd grown up with in the mountains. Best of all, though, were the moments they spent sitting on the edge of the porch just appreciating the night.

He had always loved these desert nights and had appreciated them on his own. Clear and cool, the sky was always black as tar and spangled with millions of twinkling stars, against which the surrounding mountains stood silhouetted. The pale sand stretched between them, shadowed by the clumps and streaks of vegetation. Once, when they sat together looking at the stars, he told her how it was almost as bright as daylight beneath a full moon and how sometimes in winter a light snowfall would blanket the ground and render the same effect, only to be gone by morning, as if it had been a figment of the imagination. He told her, too, of sleeping beside a camp fire and feeling all alone in the world and securely held by it at the same time. He would put his arm around her, and she would lay her head on his shoulder, and he would talk and talk and talk, more than he'd ever talked to anyone in his life. He told her stories of spring roundup, when he hired on nine or ten extra men and contracted with a chuck wagon cook to follow them around and feed them while they drove his cattle across his desert range or roped and dragged them out of the canyons, crannies and crevices of his mountains so they could be separated, treated, tagged, cut, branded and penned for shipping to market as warranted. She listened as if every word was the most interesting one she'd ever heard.

She did some talking, too. She told him about the mountains back home, the dangers of mining, the brutal lack of jobs and the hard life there. She spoke fondly and worriedly of her younger brothers, bitterly of her father, wistfully of her mother and honestly of her late husband. She described Dodie and related colorful stories about the spunky old woman who had become almost a second mother to her. They were poor folk, she told him, never knowing any other way but living hand-to-mouth. It wasn't so bad, really, she said, as long as everybody shared the hardship, but Chintz Esterbridge was not the sort to deny himself anything, no matter the expense to his family. Leon hugged her and told her that she was well out of that household, then, and she turned her face into the hollow of his shoulder, her eyes glistening with tears. She was glad she had come, she said. It was beautiful out here, she said. She felt free and hopeful here with him, she said. He laid his cheek against the top of her head and just held her. That night's parting kiss got a little out of hand, but he went to bed happy with the knowledge that he wasn't the only one fighting to stay "sensible."

He started dreaming about the life they could build together. Then a week or so after she'd arrived, he found a steer that had fallen on its side in a deep, narrow ravine and was wedged about fifteen to twenty feet down, its legs folded under and trapped against its belly. He tried everything he could think of to drag that steer up and out of that crack in the ground, but he couldn't budge it with the hold he could get by dropping a rope around its horns or head. Desperate and bedraggled, he knew he was going to have to get help or put a bullet in that steer. Had he been on the place alone, the bullet would have been his only option, but Cassie was there, she could ride and he knew she'd help if he asked.

He rode back to the house as quickly as he dared on a tired horse. When he walked into the house, his chaps flapping and his boots tracking sand all over a floor and rug she'd cleaned with her own hands, she was sitting on the couch going through one of his magazines, her long bare legs folded beneath her. "I've got a steer trapped in a crevice 'bout forty minutes from here," he said. "You've either got to help me get it out, or I've got to kill it."

She put the magazine down and started for the bedroom on small, bare feet, tugging at the hems of her shorts. "You turn off the oven while I'm changing," she said calmly.

Time was of the essence, but he stood there and watched her until she disappeared behind the curtain. He found a cake in the oven. Not nearly done yet, he feared it would be ruined if he turned off the heat, but they couldn't leave the butane burning while they were gone. Regretfully, he turned off the flame but left the cake in the oven in hopes that the heat trapped inside would be enough to cook it thoroughly. By the time he got back to the living room, Cassie was there, tucking her shirttail into her jeans.

"You better get a long-sleeved shirt," he told her. "That sun out there'll cook you."

She grimaced. "The only thing I've got with long sleeves is a sweater."

"I'll get you one of my shirts," he said, walking toward his own bedroom. He reached into the closet and ripped one off a hanger, calling out, "Don't suppose you've got a hat."

"No."

He grabbed a floppy old felt with no discernible shape from a peg on the wall and strode back into the living room. "Try these."

She reached up for them from her seat on the couch, where she had been buckling on her sandals. He shook his head.

"I forgot you don't have any regular shoes."

She blinked at him. "It won't matter, really, will it?"

He gave her a mildly disgusted look. "Now, didn't I tell you that the stirrups would rub blisters on your bare ankles?"

She nodded, properly chastened.

"I'll get you a pair of heavy socks."

She smiled up at him, and he winked, just to let her know that he was being more teasing than scolding. He started back to his bedroom.

"Get that shirt changed." He yanked open a dresser drawer, dug down to the bottom and brought out a pair of thick woolies he wore only on the coldest winter days. "These'll have to do," he said, pushing aside the curtain on his bedroom door.

She stood there in her bra, frozen in the act of slinging on his shirt. She had magnificent breasts, and the pink flesh of her torso tapered to an unbelievably narrow waist. He forgot for the moment that they were rushing to the aid of a trapped animal. He forgot that it was the middle of the day and that he still had to saddle two fresh horses and that they were being sensible. He dropped the socks and stepped up to her, his gaze eating her alive. Her bra was obviously too small. The cups were little more than triangles of flesh-toned, paper-thin nylon that stretched to barely cover nipples that grew hard even as he watched.

For a long moment out of time, they simply stood there, then he heard her swallow and heard the swish of fabric as she slid her arms into the sleeves and drew the shirt around her. He knew that if he did not do something quickly, she would cover herself. He didn't think it, he just *knew* it, and he reacted instinctively, lifting his hands to cup and test the weight of her breasts. She went absolutely still. He felt her breath seize, felt her heart thump, felt the warm, heavy, pliant softness of her and he felt himself go hard and tight. Mesmerized, he watched his thumbs flick over the hardened nipples. She gasped and flinched slightly, so he didn't do it again, afraid he'd hurt her, afraid he'd disgust her, afraid he'd do the other things he so desperately wanted to do.

He wanted to love her, wanted to strip her bare and carry her off to the bedroom to do wild, erotic things to her, but she wasn't his yet. Of everything, he remembered that, and after he remembered that, he remembered the rest. They were being sensible. They were going to get to know each other. They were going to prove compatible first. They were supposed to be rescuing a poor steer that had gotten itself wedged into a crevice in the rocks. He had to close his eyes and grit his teeth to move his hands away. Then all he could do to keep from grabbing her and dragging her against him was to turn and walk out, muttering at the last moment that he had to saddle fresh horses.

Collapsing onto the edge of the sofa, Cassie gasped for breath as tremors rolled through her body. A hole seemed to have opened somewhere deep inside her, a hole through which hot liquid poured. She was trembling and wishing he hadn't gone and loving him because he had.

He was a good man! A strong man, the dearest, most attractive man she'd met since Jos. And truth be told, she hadn't been nearly as attracted to Jos at first as she was to Leon. It was the *idea* of Jos that had intrigued her, the notion of being loved, the thought of leaving Chintz Esterbridge's house for good, of having a home and a man of her own, a trustworthy man who actually thought she was worth his time and attention. She had learned to love Jos the man even more than she'd loved the freedom and partnership he'd represented. She had learned to treasure his touch, to revel in it, but she didn't know that she had ever craved it the way she was craving Leon's now.

She had not expected this. She had hoped to like Leon or at least to be able to put up with him. She had expected contentment at the most, tolerance at the least, and she'd had no idea what to expect from him in return. He had taken her by surprise from the very beginning with his thoughtfulness and his easy talk and his teasing and his powerful sexual lure. She had felt it the moment she'd laid eyes on him, and it had nearly swamped every decent instinct she had the first time he'd kissed her. It had threatened, in fact, to overwhelm her better judgment, and she thought it only prudent to try to limit that sort of contact between them until they'd had a chance to make some intelligent decisions as to whether or not they'd suit. But she couldn't stop thinking about him. She'd lain awake nights thinking about him. She wove fantasies around him. She imagined what it would feel like to have him touch her in the most intimate ways. Today he had touched her intimately, and she was still shaking, still longing for that touch to initiate even deeper, richer intimacies. So much so that she was amazed he could turn and walk away; she could not have if her life had depended on it, and she was very aware that he had freed them both by doing so.

She pulled the shirt together and buttoned it with trembling hands, telling herself that he needed her to be level-headed and calm now. This was her chance to prove to him how much help she could be, how much better she could make his life. This was not the time to be spinning romantic fairy tales in her head. She pulled on the socks, having removed her sandals before changing her shirt, which was probably the reason he had caught her in the act. The sandals were tight over the socks, but not uncomfortably so, and she'd have worn them even if they had been. She made a vain attempt to tuck in her shirttail—or rather, Leon's shirt tail—but there was too much of it, so she settled for tying the ends in a knot and tucking in the tails of that. Finally, she grabbed the hat and plunked it on her head, but it was much too large, so she rushed to the bathroom, quickly swept the top part of her hair into a ponytail and jammed the hat down over it. She wrinkled her nose at what she saw in the mirror. She didn't exactly make an enticing picture, but she supposed it was just as well, all things considered.

Whatever the reaction she expected from Leon, it wasn't what she got. He glanced up uneasily when she entered the barn, took one look and started laughing. She was appalled at first, but then the humor in the situation took over, and she was able to laugh, too. He tied off the cinch and left the horse to come over to her. Smiling at her, he turned up the brim of her hat and smoothed it back.

"Well, this settles it," he said. "We'll have to get you properly outfitted next time we're in town."

"That sounds like you're planning on my staying around a while," she quipped unthinkingly.

His smile faded, softened. "You planning on going anywhere any time soon?"

She looked into his fawn-brown eyes and saw herself looking back from their shiny black centers. She shook her head, and his smile returned, brightened.

"Good." He tapped a finger against the tip of her nose. "Well, that steer's waiting."

She shifted her gaze, nodded and started past him. He spun, catching her by the arm. She cocked her head inquisitively, heart pounding.

"About what happened back there in the house—" he began awkwardly, then paused, dropping her arm.

She fought back the wave of heat that threatened to bring color to her cheeks, and lifted her chin. "What about it?"

He opened his mouth, closed it, laid a finger beside his nose consideringly and finally directed his gaze to hers again. "I was going to say that I'm sorry...but I'm not, and you might as well know it."

She blinked at him. "Oh."

"So if you're expecting an apology, just forget it because I think it's more important to be honest, and—"

"I do, too."

"Frankly, I think it's important that a man and a woman in our situation be attracted to each other, or—"

"Yes, I agree."

"—there's just no point in carrying on. We wouldn't be happy together, and besides I want a family, so—"

"You do?" she exclaimed happily, clapping her hands together in surprise and delight.

He looked blank for a moment. "I do what?"

"Want a family, kids, I mean."

He narrowed his eyes as if to say she'd lost what little sense God had given her. "I just said so, didn't I?"

"You did!"

"Naturally I did. You think I want to leave this place to somebody else's kids? 'Course, if I had to, there's Dale's boys, but he's going to leave the Far Gone to them, so I might as well have my own, don't you think?"

"Yes, I do!" She was so happy, she was laughing.

"Good. I mean...you like kids, don't you?"

"Of course!"

He held his hand out to her and smiled. "Well, that's one thing we've got in common," he said softly, "or should I say two?"

Cassie could scarcely breathe. The perfection of it, the perfection of *him,* swept over her in one thrilling wave of certainty. She put her hand in his and let him pull her to him, thinking of Petey and Barton, Freddy and the twins. Technically, Newt wasn't a child any longer, but he'd be lots of help around the place, and Leon was bound to see that, once she pointed it out. Suddenly, her heart felt as though it were going to burst wide open with joy, and she jerked away impulsively to throw her arms around his neck. His eyebrows shot up and he caught her to him, laughing and swinging her around in a circle.

"If you like the idea that much," he said, "maybe we ought to get started!"

"Started?" she echoed laughingly.

He steadied them and drew her close, his hands dropping to her waist. "Making babies."

Babies! Of course, he would want babies! His own babies. But that didn't mean he wouldn't want *her* boys. Did it? He curled his hand beneath her chin and tilted her head back, his own descending slowly, when all at once the other implication of that last statement hit her. Babies. *Making* babies! She gulped, mentally backpedaling even as her body warmed to the idea, and her thoughts stumbled over the pertinent word.

"Steer," she said, his mouth a finger's width above hers.

He went dead still, then abruptly pulled back and started spouting Spanish. "Get on that horse!" he said, kissing her quickly.

Fighting a grin, she nodded briskly and hurried to do as she was told. The trim little sorrel gelding he'd saddled for her stood obediently while Cassie hiked her leg up and crawled into the saddle. Leon fetched a coil of rope and tied it to the side jockey of her saddle with the wang strings near the front, then tucked a pulley into the saddlebags he'd tied on the rear. He tossed her a pair of gloves, then tugged on one of his own and mounted up with the other clamped in his teeth. He backed his big dun out of the stall and headed it toward the door, glancing back over his shoulder.

"We're going to ride fast, darlin', so try to keep up. But you're more important than the steer, so if you're having trouble, sing out, now. Hear?"

She nodded confidently, maneuvering her own mount into position behind him. He winked and touched his heels to the dun's flanks. Muscles rippled beneath the sleek gray-brown coat and the horse shot forward. Cassie's sorrel trotted after it, then once free of the barn broke into an easy lope. Leon looked over his shoulder to check her progress and, apparently satisfied, urged the dun on faster. Mindful of the many small holes, rocks and other unseen obstacles that he had explained could cause a horse to stumble, she kept the sorrel right in Leon's tracks, though in truth the animal showed no inclination to hare off on its own, anyway.

After several minutes, they slowed to a walk, then a little later sped up again. In this way, Leon explained, they could keep from blowing the horses, that is, wearing them out so completely that they were oxygen-depleted from shortness of breath. A blown horse, he said, could drop in its tracks, a dangerous experience for both horse and rider. Cassie nodded her understanding and concentrated on keeping her seat. By the time they started climbing, she was merely hanging on, exhausted from trying to remember and do all that Leon had taught her.

They heard the steer bawling well before they reached the plateau of rock split by the crevice. Leon pulled up and dismounted, tethering the horse to a scrubby shrub that pushed up between two huge boulders.

"Sounds strong," he said, pulling blocks of wood and enormous nuts and bolts from his saddlebags. "Hope he hasn't done any damage to himself. Don't think he could, really, he's wedged in there so tight."

Cassie slid down to the ground, wincing at the pangs and aches she felt. "Anything I can do?"

"Loosen up those muscles some," he said, lining up holes and sliding iron rods into place. "I'm going to need you down in that ravine directly."

Her mouth dropped open. "Me?"

He nodded.

"Why me?"

He was sliding bolts into place and screwing on nuts. "'Cause you can't pull me back up."

"Oh." Seemed reasonable. She shook out her legs and strolled over to the edge of the crack to take a peek. What she saw had her gasping and scrambling back to firmer footing. "It's a fifty-foot drop!"

"Naw," he said, "it's not more than fifteen, maybe twenty."

Oh, is that all! she thought, pushing up her sleeves.

He seemed to read her thoughts. "You'll be okay. I'll get you down and up again with no problem. Hard part's going to be getting that rope around the critter."

She put her hands to her head in shock. "You want me to put a rope around a steer wedged in a crack twenty feet down in the ground?"

He looked up at her, eyes squinted. "Yep, that's about all there is to it."

"Leon! I can't do this! It's impossible!"

"Now don't get all negative," he said, walking over to her horse to get the pulley he'd put in her saddlebags. "Just do as I tell you and have a little faith, okay?" He took the coil of rope, too, looping it over his shoulder.

She watched him walk to a spot about two yards away where two rock surfaces came together, one slightly higher than the other. He wedged the little tripod he'd made into the crack between two surfaces, fixed the pulley to it and began threading the rope through the gear, his movements sure and confident. She relaxed a bit. "I guess you've done this before, huh?"

"Not exactly."

She coiled her hands into nervous fists. "Well, which is it? Not or exactly?"

He sent her a look from beneath the jut of his eyebrows. "Listen," he said evenly, "if you don't want to do this, just say so, because if you don't, then the sooner I put the poor thing out of its misery the better."

She gulped. "Wh-what do you mean by that?"

He stood and placed his hands on his hips. "Aren't any other options. You wouldn't want me to leave it down there to starve to death, would you?"

"Good Lord, no!"

"Well, then?"

"Well...." She closed her eyes briefly. There really wasn't any other acceptable option; anyway, she knew Leon wouldn't let anything happen to her. She pushed her shoulders back. "What do I do first?"

He smiled and nodded with satisfaction. "Get those gloves on, then come here."

She did exactly as he told her every step of the way, raising her arms and spreading her legs so he could fashion a halter for her from the rope, paying close attention as he showed her how to carry the second coil over her shoulder and how to enlarge the loop he'd made in the end of it, listening intently as he described how she'd have to brace her legs on the sides of the ravine when she got down to the steer, then work the loop over its hind legs, careful to keep clear of the thrashing horns.

"It won't be able to kick you," he explained, "because there isn't room, but it might shift some and pin an arm, a hand or a foot against the rock. If that happens, you stay calm and work free. Worse comes to worse, I'll shoot that sucker in the head, then I'll take the other end of the rope and come down to get you. All right?"

She nodded, but she was thinking that she'd be damned if she'd go down there, risk injury or worse and then let him shoot the creature. He gave her a quick hug and a swat on the rear, then moved into position. Sitting behind the tripod, he grasped the rope in his gloved hands, then braced his legs. "When you get to the steer, give a holler. I'll slack up and tie off. Once the other rope's around the animal, you just keep a hold of the end. I'll pull you up first, then we'll use the horses to get the steer out. Understood?"

She nodded once more.

"Let's get to it," he said.

Reluctantly, she walked to the edge of the ravine and sat down, scooting over the lip on her bottom as he'd instructed. The gully was too wide near the top to allow her any purchase at all with her legs and feet, but the rope held tight, and the ravine soon narrowed enough so that she could awkwardly brace one foot on either side and inch her way down. The steer huffed and bawled as she lowered toward it. She tried talking to it in a calm, comforting voice, but it struggled and thrashed and tried to drown her out with frantic calls of its own. Just above it, she wedged her feet in tight and yelled up to Leon. He threw her some slack and seconds later appeared belly down at the edge of the ravine. He was saying something, but she couldn't hear him for the bawling of the steer. He cupped his hands and yelled, "Kick it!"

"What?"

"Kick that damned thing in the butt!"

Rolling her eyes, she braced her hands on the sides of the ravine, shifted the weight off her feet and thumped the steer on the rump. Leon cupped his hands again and shouted down to her.

"You can't hurt it, Cassie. Haul off and pound that sucker!"

She curled her toes back in her sandal, drew down and whacked the animal. It shut up like somebody had flipped a switch. Cassie looked up at Leon with new respect.

"Easy now, sweetheart," he said, "I don't want any broken bones in that luscious body of yours."

She gave him a dry glance and went to work. Thirty sweaty minutes later, she was almost ready to shoot that steer herself, but she finally got both rear hooves in that loop, worked it up over the legs and wedged it around the flank. "That's the best I can do, Leon," she shouted up to him, wiping dirty streaks across her face with the back of her hand. "You'll have to try to pull it farther up his body from up there."

"Hang on, honey, and I'll get you out of there," he said, disappearing from view.

Her legs and arms trembling, she couldn't help him much on the way up, just catch herself every time the rope stopped so she wouldn't bang against the sides of the ravine. But he didn't seem to have much trouble, and she was at the top almost before she was ready, scrabbling to pull herself over the edge. He tied off the rope and came to help her, a canteen of water in one hand. He pulled her up between his legs, eased back from the edge and hauled her up to her feet, his arms going around her as she swayed unsteadily. He brushed the coils of rope off her shoulder and dropped them to the ground.

"I don't know if it's going to work, Leon," she told him, shaking her head, but his concern seemed to be for her.

"Sit down now, baby, and let me and the horses do the rest. You did your best, and that's all anybody can do, so put your mind at ease."

She nodded and let him ease her to the ground once more. She swigged water while he untied her harness and rigged up the horses. "I don't want you to shoot him, Leon," she said, "but I don't know if it's going to work."

He walked over to where she sat, pushed her hat back and bent down. "Tell you what," he said with a wink, "since you're so attached to that stupid beast, if we have to shoot him, we won't eat him. Now, does that make you feel better?"

"Oh, swell, Leon!" she exclaimed, twisting the cap back onto the canteen.

He laughed and kissed her in the middle of the forehead. "I'll have to teach you to cuss in Spanish," he said and walked off.

She flopped down prone onto the ground, and concentrated on the exquisite pleasure of simply not having her muscles in a strain. Her muscle tone had improved some from riding, but this episode had been tough work. It seemed like forever before Leon got everything ready and started walking the horses forward. Then the moment the rope tightened, the steer started to bellow again. Cassie scrambled over to the edge and stretched out on her belly.

"You're hurting him!"

"Honey, I'm probably killing him!" he yelled. "Which ends pointing up?"

"Neither!"

He said something in Spanish and started clucking his tongue at the horses. The rope shifted, and then the steer.

"What's happening?"

"He's moving!"

"Which end?"

"The head, I think!"

He mumble something in Spanish and started clucking his tongue at the horses. The rope shifted and then the steer.

Cassie held her breath as the steer bawled, and bawled, and then it was kicking, its rear end sliding downward. Suddenly, it was scrambling toward her. "It's coming! It's coming!" she screamed.

Leon was running downhill in front of the horses. "Get out of there!" he yelled. "Move it! Move it!"

She glanced down into the ravine, and that steer was right there, its crazed eyes fastened on her face, horns churning. She threw her arms over her head and pitched backward, just as it came over the edge, snorting and throwing its head. A hoof clipped her on the hip and then it was gone in a clatter of rocks. When she looked up next, Leon was in the saddle, the rope in both hands. The steer and the sorrel were lighting out in different directions. Then something remarkable happened. The dun seemed to dig in. A split second later, Leon whipped the rope, and the loop around the steer's body loosened. It kicked free and loped off down the slope, bawling and flicking its tail. Leon calmly sat back in the saddle and started coiling his rope. Cassie gaped and started to laugh. He looped the rope over his saddle horn, turned the horse and trotted back in her direction.

"We did it!" she cried, leaping to her feet and waving her hat over her head.

He dismounted and came toward her, the reins in one hand. "Never doubted we would," he claimed, eyes dancing. "We make a pretty good team, don't you think?"

"We do!" she crowed. "We do!"

"Hold this," he said, handing over the reins with a grin. In her elation, she sputtered words, replaying the whole effort while he quickly broke apart the tripod and pulley, coiled up the other rope and fixed everything in place around the saddle. He had taken the reins from her hand and was swinging up onto the dun again before she realized she was without a mount.

"What are we going to do?" she wailed.

He reached down and hauled her up into the saddle in front of him.

"But what about my horse?"

"He'll probably beat us back to the barn," he said unconcernedly.

She laughed and laid her head on his shoulder, catching her hat as it tumbled off. "Why didn't I think of that?"

"You're too happy to think," he said, wrapping his arm around her, "but I'm not."

"You're not? How come?"

"Because," he said, "you just wanted that dumb steer up out of that hole, and that's what you got, but I want something else."

The sound of his voice warned her, but she couldn't quite believe it. She turned her head and tilted it back to look up at him. "What is it you want, Leon?" she asked breathlessly.

He glanced down at her, then back up to stare straight ahead. For a long while he didn't answer, then he shifted slightly, and his arm tightened around her. "There's a three day waiting period," he said softly. "If we get the license tomorrow, we can do it on Friday and spend the weekend...well, celebrating. We need to do a little shopping, too, of course. I think that's in order, don't you?"

She didn't say a word, afraid she wasn't hearing what she thought she was hearing. He went on.

"If you want a preacher, there's one we can call. A priest, too, for that matter." She sat up straight and turned as far as she could in the saddle. He ignored her. "I could call Dolores and Cutter and ask them to stand up for us," he said, "and in case you haven't figured it out, I'm asking you to marry me."

It was true! She lifted her hands to her face, tears starting. "Oh, Leon!" she whispered.

He looked at her, eyes shining. "You said it yourself," he told her softly. "We make a pretty good team, and I think I'm one lucky *hijo de un perro* if you say yes." He stopped the horse and pulled her around to face him. "You are going to say yes, aren't you?"

Her heart was in her throat, so she just nodded, tears rolling down her cheeks.

"I swear," he said in a choked voice, "you're wearing half of Texas on your face." And he kissed her like she'd never been kissed before, Texas and all.

Chapter Four

Cassie woke to the sunlight pouring through the window, and her first thought was that she was going to be married. Her second was that she'd overslept. Leon generally had breakfast before dawn. She turned over, peacefully aware of the triangle of sunlight on the narrow brick floor of her room, and felt a twinge of pain. She was not surprised, considering yesterday's exertions. It was much worse than she'd feared, however. Just sitting up on the creaky bed and swinging her legs over the side brought untold agony. Pain shot up her calves and thighs into her hips and back, and her arms felt like lead weights. She cried out as she got to her feet, her muscles stiff as wood.

Leon pushed aside the curtain and stepped through the door, a cup of coffee in his hand. His gaze slid over her. She was properly covered in an old T-shirt and a pair of knit shorts, but she felt absurdly exposed. She smiled lamely, put a hand to the small of her back and tried to stretch the kinks out. It was the wrong thing to do. He watched with undisguised interest the outward, upward thrust of her breasts. She immediately slumped forward, her grimace only partly legitimate. His fawn-colored eyes twinkled knowingly.

"Pretty sore this morning, I expect," he said, lifting his cup to his lips.

She nodded, embarrassed. "I overslept. Sorry."

"No problem. Or did you forget that we're going into town today?"

Town. The marriage license. The embarrassment left her, but an unexpected shyness took its place. She shook her head, unaware of the softness of her gaze. "I didn't forget."

He smiled. "Good. Want some breakfast?"

"Oh, you must be starving!" she exclaimed.

He shook his head. "Nope. I've already eaten. Yours is in the warming oven."

"I'm really sorry," she told him, tottering stiffly through the door.

He followed her into the living room. "Why? I can cook, you know. Besides, you're in no shape for it this morning."

"I know," she groaned, grasping the back of the chair and leaning on it for support. "What am I going to do?"

"Well, first," he said, putting down his cup, "we're going to loosen up those muscles. Come here."

She crept over to him, a hand pressed to the small of her back.

"Turn around."

Just that much movement caused twinges of pain, but she complied. It didn't even occur to her not to. Leon laid his hands upon her shoulders. They were warm and heavy and, when he began to massage her, instruments of torture.

"Oh! Ah! Ow!"

"Got to work it out, hon. Only way."

She lifted a hand to the back of her neck and nodded. Now, how the devil had she gotten sore there? she wondered, but then she thought of herself bent over that struggling steer, her legs braced against the sides of that ravine, the ropes cutting into her shoulders and the bends of her hips. She moaned. "Even the soles of my feet hurt."

"It'll get better, sooner than you think."

"I hope so."

Actually, her shoulders were already beginning to feel more relaxed and flexible. She moved them to be sure and sighed with relief at the diminished pain. He moved his hands down her back, working and heating the muscles. She leaned forward slightly, easing his access. When he'd worked his way down to her buttocks, he dropped onto his haunches. She thought he meant to skip that part and begin with her legs, so when he covered her cheeks with his big hands and began to knead, she stiffened, and pain shot downward into her legs. "Ow!"

"Relax," he ordered.

She put her head down and took a deep breath, consciously loosening her muscles, but his every touch brought new stiffening—and hot melting in other quarters. Color suffused her face, and she was thankful for the curtain of her hair hanging forward. Then he slid his hand between her legs, and she gasped.

"Spread," he commanded, his voice thick and husky.

She should have refused, but she didn't. She wanted him to touch her, and it had little to do with the thought that he would soon be her husband. She would have wanted this, she realized, whether he had proposed marriage or not, and she was shocked. She had not expected to want him; all she had expected was not to be repelled, but she realized suddenly that she had wanted him to touch her almost from the beginning—and her behavior had surely shown it. She almost laughed, knowing now that, without ever having formed the thought, she had believed she was somehow seducing *him* into wanting *her*. Then his fingers grazed the sensitive area at the juncture of her thighs and she spasmed with the intensity of the sensation, a sound emitting from low in her throat. He said not a word, merely moved his hand to massage the tendon in the bend of her leg, his knuckles continually brushing against her.

It was agony, sheer hell, and it was bliss, the most inflaming kind of bliss. She had forgotten that it could be like this. It was thrilling. It was heady. He began working his way down her leg, strong fingers squeezing and stretching sore muscles. She was swallowing air through her mouth, trying desperately to still her clamoring body. When he got down to her ankle, he lifted her leg, bent it backward at the knee and rested her shin upon his thigh. Deftly he manipulated her foot, loosening the ankle, then dug his thumbs into the arch of her foot and began to massage there. It was the most splendid sensation she had ever felt, the most soothing, relaxing touch imaginable, and it turned her instantly to mush. She had to reach out and press a hand to the wall to keep from collapsing.

"You like that," he said softly, silkily.

She could only moan in affirmation.

After a long while, he moved to the other foot. It felt so good, so warm and intimate and—loving. She had never expected to feel loved again. Tears rose in her eyes. Was it possible? Could she have it, loving and being loved, a second time? Was God that good, that generous? It almost seemed too much to ask, but oh, what hope she had suddenly! To be more than one side of a bargain, a convenience to make an inconvenient life somehow easier. And she hadn't even told him the truth! He didn't know that she couldn't come to him alone. He didn't know that she wanted something more from him than he wanted from her. Dear God, how could she tell him now? He would be hurt. He would be shocked. Betrayed. What had she done?

His hands moved to her ankle, then quickly higher. Pain returned, not nearly so intense now, not nearly so sharp. She could have wished for more, anything to drive these thoughts out of her head. What could she do? *What could she do?* She had to tell him, but how could she? How could she bear to hurt him? She had to tell him. She'd rather go, change her mind, leave him now before he realized what she'd done. But how was she to know that he might actually fall in love with her? Why would he love her? A man like Leon.

Or Jos. A man like Jos.

She was stunned. Something about her could make two good men love her. And she was a liar, a fraud, a user. She thought of her father and felt physically ill. She could not go through with this. She would leave. Today. He was taking her to town. Once there, she could tell him that she had changed her mind and ask him for bus fare—where? She could not even go back to the boys, for the boys were with Chintz. All but Petey. Could she and Petey stay with Dodie? Dodie needed her help. She could do more, and her pay could be room and board for herself and her son. But that would mean the boys would have to stay with Chintz and Marlene or more likely go into the welfare system. It couldn't be helped, she told herself fiercely.

Freddy's wiseacre smile and Barton's bottle-thick glasses floated before her mind's eye. How could she leave them to Chintz? How would they survive the growing brutality she knew they would face? And what of the twins? They were scamps already. How much more would it take for them to become like their father? And Newt. Newt deserved better. He was brilliant, dogged and frustrated. He would take his fists to Chintz again and again—until Chintz killed him. Or vice versa. And neither was acceptable.

She couldn't go back. She didn't want to go back. The only other thing she could do then was to love Leon Paradise with all her heart and soul. And body. He was making her so very aware of what it would mean to love him with her body. She almost welcomed the pain when he began to massage the other tendon at the apex of her thighs, but there was the stroking of his knuckles, too, more pronounced this time, unless she was losing her mind, and that might very well be. She was breathing through her mouth

again, gasping, shuddering, not even trying to hide her reaction. Her mind was made up now. She couldn't stop,
couldn't go back. She had to tell him, gently, delicately,
slowly. She had to make him know that she could love him,
would love him, *did* love him with every fiber of her being.

When he turned his hand and cupped her, she knew the
pretense was over. She arched against his palm. He moved
close and rose, dragging his body against hers, pressing her
to the wall. He rubbed his hand back and forth over her.
She put her head back, gasping, undulating. He nuzzled her
ear through the silky curtain of her hair. "God, I wish you
weren't too sore."

"I'm not."

He brushed back her hair with his free hand and set his
teeth in the sensitive flesh of her neck. "I don't want to hurt
you," he whispered, then trailed his tongue upward to the
lobe of her ear.

"You won't. You couldn't."

"I want to make love to you."

"I want that, too, but...." Gently. Slowly.

He took his hand away and turned her to face him. "I'll
wait," he said. "Friday's not so far away."

She gazed into his soft brown eyes. "I have to tell you
something."

He put his forehead to hers. "Good." He lifted his head
and kissed her between the eyes. "What?" He smiled at
her, so sure, so strong. He lifted his hands to cup her face.
"Tell me."

She swallowed the lump in her throat. Her heart was
pounding so hard, she thought she might collapse. Petey.
At least, she had to tell him about Petey, but what if he was
angry, disappointed? What if he could not accept another
man's son? What hope would there be then—for any of
them? He saw the fear in her face and grew solemn.

"You're trembling," he said softly. "Cassie? Honey?"

"I have a son!" she blurted out. "He's four. I should
have told you right from the start. I don't why I didn't! I

never thought it would come to this. I never dared hope...."

He dropped his hands, incredulity lifting his eyebrows and rounding his mouth. "You have a son?"

She couldn't tell what he was thinking, feeling, beyond the surprise. She leaned against the wall, arms crossing her chest as if she could somehow hold herself together should he turn away. She didn't know what else to say. What else should she say? He put his hands to his hips.

"You have a son." He shook his head. "You thought that would make a difference? You thought I wouldn't want you if I knew?"

She opened her mouth, closed it, nodded.

He stepped close and placed a hand on either side of her head. He was looking at her mouth. "Maybe it would have at first," he told her honestly. "Not now."

Relief washed over her, but she couldn't help thinking that it might have been different if she'd told him the truth at the very beginning.

"Where is he?" Leon asked.

She gulped. "With Dodie. I couldn't leave him with Pa. Marlene slaps him, but he's a good boy, quiet, shy."

"What's his name?"

"Peter Josiah."

"After his father, I presume."

"Yes. I—I call him Petey."

"Will he like me, do you think?" he asked gently. "Will he like it out here?"

She looked into his face. "Oh, Leon," she whispered.

He put his head down and kissed her. She could scarcely contain the feelings that surged through her, the gratitude, the relief, the desire—the love, for she had no doubt that she was in love, none at all.

She wrapped her arms around his neck and pushed her body against him. He embraced her, his mouth working hers. She wanted him, needed him, now, this very minute. Every movement brought a slight pain, soreness in every muscle, but she didn't care. It wasn't real, not as real as him.

He broke the kiss, panting lightly in her ear. "You didn't answer."

She couldn't even remember the question!

"Will he be happy here, your son?"

That question! "Yes. Oh, yes, I'm sure of it."

"Will he accept me?"

"Of course he will!"

"We'll send for him today."

Today! Elation swept through her. He was willing to send for Petey today, to bring him here, to raise him! But Petey was just one little boy. There were five others he had to know about. He'd said that he wanted a family, but what man in his right mind would want six half grown boys? Still, she had to tell him. Didn't she? She couldn't abandon her brothers; she had promised them a home, but that didn't mean she had to tell him *this moment.* She would tell him later, when his mouth wasn't seeking hers, when this need was assuaged, when he knew how much she loved him. That was her only hope, really, to convince him first that she loved him, to make him love her. And to think she'd conceived this as a sort of bargain! Who would have guessed there would be such happiness, such excitement to share? It was she who broke the kiss this time.

"How can I ever thank you!"

He shook his head. "I don't want you to thank me."

"What do you want? I'll give it to you. Anything."

"Everything," he said softly. "I want it all for us, Cass, everything two people can have between them. That's what I want, and starting Friday, I'll get it. I really believe that."

She tightened her arms about his neck, and pressed herself against him. "We don't have to wait."

He grinned and kissed the tip of her nose. "Yeah, we do. I believe a thing worth doing is worth doing right, and I think you do, too, but I'm gratified to know you're as tempted as I am."

A wave of wonder shimmered through her. She looked into his soft brown eyes, a smile curving her mouth. "Oh, Leon," she said. "Oh, Leon, I'm so lucky! How did I ever get so lucky?"

"Maybe it was just time for a change of luck," he said. "For both of us."

They got a late start, but by early evening they were the proud owners of a marriage license, a pair of plain gold wedding bands and a receipt for two bus tickets from West Virginia to Texas. Petey was obviously too young to travel alone, so it was decided that Newt would make the trip with him. Leon said affably that he'd welcome a visit with Cassie's artistic brother. After all, they were going to be family very soon. Cassie casually suggested that Newt could be of help to Leon around the place, but Leon pointed out that the house was not really big enough for more than the two of them and Petey. When he could get around to it, he'd add on to the place, he said. Cassie remarked that the house was really no bigger than what she, Petey, all her brothers, Chintz and Marlene had been living in, but she did not push the matter. Her happiness dimmed a bit, but she hoped that Leon would come to like Newt so well and find him such a help that Leon himself would insist Newt stay. After that, she could carefully reveal the others, stating how desperately the twins needed taking in hand. And then, it should be relatively easy to convince him to take in Freddy and Bart. She wouldn't believe that he couldn't be convinced, that he wouldn't help.

She enclosed a quickly penned letter to Newt with the bus tickets, all of which she sent in care of Dodie. She told her brother of her impending wedding, and she assured him that Leon was a wonderful man. It was only a matter of time, she told him, before they could all be together again. She would have liked to have told him what a lovely place the Paradise was, but the mail carrier was waiting for her to finish so he could post the letter and close up shop. Afterward, Cassie and Leon had dinner in a barbecue restaurant and drove back out to the ranch.

The next day was imbued with anticipation. Leon still rode out before daylight, but breakfast and dinner were accompanied with long, lingering kisses, and they spent the evening side by side on the sofa or with him sitting in the arm chair and she on his lap. They were careful not to let things get out of hand, but oh! the temptation was delicious. They discussed the wedding, deciding that simple was best. Leon surprised her by preferring a minister; she happily agreed, and he made the arrangements via telephone. The first order of business was to inform his friends. Cutter and Dolores Patterson, were understandably shocked but properly enthusiastic in their congratulations. They insisted that the ceremony take place in their own living room. Since Cassie would have been happy to marry Leon on a street corner with a stop sign as witness, she couldn't have cared less, but Leon seemed truly pleased. It was decided that the ceremony would take place late in the afternoon to allow them time to shop for wedding clothes and get dressed. Saying good-night was a long, drawn out affair that left her trembling with desire and unable to sleep for hours.

Nevertheless, she came awake Friday morning while the dawn was still new and slipped into the kitchen to find Leon already dressed and drinking a cup of coffee. He came up out of his chair with a whoop, caught her around the waist, and whirled her around the room, as if his joy was simply too great to contain. Laughing, she wrapped her arms around his neck and kissed him. He sat down in his chair again with her in his lap.

"Hungry?"

She shook her head. "Too nervous, I think, but I'll fix you something."

"Nah, I was thinking about a late breakfast at Sophie's."

"Sounds good. I'll hurry and get dressed."

"In a minute," he said and proceeded to kiss her silly.

The sun was high by the time they reached Van Horn. They feted themselves at Sophía's, smiling secretively into each other's eyes, then they checked into a local motel for the weekend, both fully aware of what was to come. It was a surprisingly nice motel considering the size of the community, and Cassie's very first experience with such. Leon was pleased that she was impressed and decided aloud that on their first anniversary he was going to take her to a "really fine" hotel in El Paso. Just the mention of their first anniversary brought tears to her eyes. He laughed at her and kissed her right there in the lobby of the motel, and then he took her shopping.

Leon was determined to "outfit" Cassie. Over her objections, he bought her several pairs of the "right" jeans, some exquisitely tailored shirts, and two pairs of boots, one pearl white for "dress" and a more mundane pair for everyday. He bought her two hats, as well, a white felt with an angora finish and a good, serviceable beaver. Even then he wasn't done. She wanted something special to get married in, didn't she? After much careful consideration and many changes of clothing, she settled on a long wrap skirt of Indian print in tones of white, cream, and tan, with a matching vest and a white blouse. Leon settled on a white denim miniskirt and waistlength jacket with a bright green elastic tube top. To her dismay they wound up with both.

She tried to tell him that for her part she'd rather spend less money on clothing and more on other things, such as paint for the house and one or two bright rugs to replace that brown thing on the living room floor. His answer was to escort her post haste to a store that sold both. When she dug in her heels and refused to choose colors, he did so himself, choosing the most outrageous combinations possible. She quickly stepped in and set him straight—and left hauling gallon buckets, quarts, and pints of various hues, along with several sizes of brushes and rollers.

Cassie was appalled at the amount of money they had spent that day, but Leon was in fine fettle. "You were saving to buy that extra 8,000 acres," she argued.

He kissed the top of her head. "That extra acreage is good as bought," he said lightly, "soon as I get around to it. Right now I've got to make provision for my family."

My family. She smiled and lifted her mouth to his. "Do you know how wonderful you are?" she whispered.

"I'm the luckiest wonderful fellow around," he said and kissed her. It only occurred to them when they heard the honking car horns and laughter that they were standing on the sidewalk.

A glance at Leon's watch put him in high gear. He declared that they had just enough time to deliver their purchases to the motel and get to the Pattersons' in time to dress. The wedding wasn't scheduled to take place until six, some four hours yet, but if Leon said they ought to hurry, she figured they ought to hurry. They were at the Pattersons' within a quarter hour.

Cutter Patterson was a local banker, and his house was a long, low, pale brick affair with a white shingled roof and black wrought iron grill work. The drive was dirt and the lawn consisted of a patch of brownish, downbeaten grass. A tiny concrete pad in the back served as a patio, and a big, white, boxy, domestic luxury car took up every available inch of the car port. Patterson's wife Dolores answered the door. She was a tall, slender woman with the flawless dark skin of her Mexican mother and the thick, reddish brown hair and blue eyes of her Caucasian father. She beamed at them and threw her arms first around Leon and then Cassie. "Come in, come in. You're just in time."

"Just in time for what?" Leon asked, ushering Cassie through the doorway just abandoned by Dolores Patterson.

"Lunch," she called over her shoulder as she swayed gracefully down the entry hall and into the living room.

"Set two more places, honey!" she shouted, "and use paper. I don't want to wash dishes all day."

Leon and Cassie caught up with her in the living room. She spread her arms and looked around her. "What do you think?"

Cassie had never seen such a nice house. The room was large and cool, the carpeting, walls, and furniture a surprisingly rosy pink accented with bits of turquoise and creamy white. There were large, pottery based lamps, heavy plank tables, and a ceiling fan circling lazily above them. A white brick fireplace occupied the inside wall and above the rough hewn mantel hung a mirror at least six feet wide and four feet tall with a hammered tin frame flanked by matching sconces. There were bouquets of flowers everywhere, on the mantel and tables and one large basket standing before the screen in front of the fireplace.

"You didn't have to do this!" Leon exclaimed.

Cutter Patterson appeared in a door to their immediate left. He wore dark, sharply creased blue jeans and a white, long sleeved western shirt with a black string tie. He seemed older than Leon, his hair more silver than blond, and carried a bit of extra weight around his middle. His face was too round to be classically handsome, but he had a pleasant look about him and sharp intelligent hazel eyes. He was grinning. "You think we'd let you get married without making a fuss? Besides, when did you ever know Dolores to pass up a chance to shop? She was in El Paso this morning before the stores opened. She bought out one whole flower shop. Most fun she's had in months."

"Ooh, and I got you a wonderful wedding present!" Dolores exclaimed, admitting all. "It's a set of dishes, heavy stoneware stuff done by the Indians in...well, I don't remember where. Come on, I'll show you. I was going to wrap it, but what the heck, you already know what it is." She led the way into the kitchen as she revealed all. The dishes were sitting in their big box on the counter. They were heavy, brick red with a narrow circle of yellow in the center and a wide band of turquoise blue on the outside edge. Cassie loved them instantly. She'd never had a whole set of matched dishes in her life. Caught up in the wonder of it, she hugged a plate to her chest, eyes tearing.

"Thanks, Dolores, Cutter," Leon said, his hands falling comfortingly on Cassie's shoulders.

"Yes, thank you," she said, sniffing.

"Honey," Dolores replied, "it was my pleasure. Believe me, I live to shop."

Cassie managed a chuckle. "Well, you and Leon must get along fine, then. He's been spending money all morning like water."

Dolores raised her eyebrows. "I'm impressed."

"Yeah," Leon said, "I even bought a pair of new jeans to get married in, so lead me to the starch. Got to look good for my wedding."

"Laundry room's through there," Dolores announced, pointing toward a pair of slatted swinging doors. "I keep a sink full of starch all the time," she told Cassie. "Banker's got to look his best every day."

"What's it for?" Cassie asked innocently.

Dolores looked surprised. "Why, to give body to his jeans, of course, get those creases razor sharp."

Cassie looked at the jeans folded like cardboard in Leon's arms. "But they're already so stiff."

Dolores folded her arms, eyebrows arched. "Sugar, if you can move in them they aren't stiff enough by cowboy standards." She sucked in a nonexistent gut and pulled her rib cage up high, patting her flat tummy. "Personally, I like them stiff 'cause they hold you in, you know?" She cocked her head. "Then again, you don't need much holding in, do you?"

"More than you!" Cassie retorted.

Dolores sparkled. "I knew we were going to be friends."

They both laughed, and Leon left them to starch his jeans stiff as lumber. Dolores sat down at the table and invited Cassie to join her, while Cutter went about preparing a lunch of fried bacon and cheese sandwiches. What followed was a casual grilling that had nothing whatsoever to do with cooking. Dolores asked questions without the slightest compunction and Cassie answered them as carefully as possible. Within minutes she had disclosed everything she dared and was explaining her father's second marriage.

Dolores tossed her hair when Cassie was through and hooked one elbow over the back of her chair. "The old lecher, knocking up a seventeen-year-old girl!"

Cassie nodded. "Marlene isn't exactly blameless," she said, "though what she'd want with my pa is beyond me. He's a heavy shiner, moonshine, that is, booze."

Dolores snorted. "Maybe she'll leave him soon as something better catches her eye," she said.

"More likely the other way around," Cassie said. "I never could figure it out, but women just fall over him."

"Sounds like Cutter," Dolores muttered. Cassie stilled in shock, intensely aware that he was standing right behind her. Dolores waved a hand negligently. "Oh, don't get me wrong. He doesn't fool around. He wouldn't dare, but that doesn't keep the women from throwing themselves at him. Honestly, nothing makes a man so attractive as a little money. Now Leon, he doesn't need money—for anything that I can tell. How'd you two meet, anyway?"

Cassie felt her face flame. "Well, uh...."

"I ran a personal ad," Leon admitted flatly from behind her. Cassie whirled around on her chair to send him a pleading stare. He shook his head faintly, then slid his gaze at Cutter. "I ran a personal ad," he repeated calmly, "in a horse breeder's magazine, and it found its way to West Virginia, where a friend of Cassie's read it and answered it on Cassie's behalf. Eventually the friend convinced Cassie to write me. We've been writing for months, and a few weeks ago I brought her out here for a visit. We decided it ought to be permanent. Actually," he went on, his gaze traveling back to Cassie, "the whole thing's worked out a lot better than I ever imagined.'' He smiled. It was a private thing, hot and full of promise, and it evoked both gratitude and love in Cassie.

She got up and went to him, slid her arms around his waist, hid her face in the hollow of his shoulder. He laid his cheek against the top of her head and hugged her tight. Neither of them saw the look that passed between Cutter and Dolores. It was a look of hope as well as concern.

Chapter Five

Cassie was dressed for the wedding long before anyone else in the house. She wandered into the living room and moved from flower arrangement to flower arrangement, sniffing the exotic perfumes and trying to quell the misgivings that were plaguing her. They had nothing to do with whether or not to marry Leon, only with the lies of omission she knew she was committing. She had promised the boys a home, and she meant to keep that promise. It had been her reason for coming to Texas in the beginning, but only in the beginning. Would Leon believe that? Better that he never knew. Better that she live with this guilt the rest of her life than disappoint him, and yet she could not escape the feeling that she *ought* to tell him. Ironically it made her feel a little better when she wandered close to the hallway and overheard enough of a conversation to know that Leon hadn't exactly told her absolutely everything either. It was Cutter who tipped her off.

"Don't you think you should at least call them afterward?" Cutter said.

"No," Leon replied. "They'll find out soon enough. I want a little time with her before they descend on us. That's not too much to ask, is it?"

"But they're you're family," Cutter argued. "Your mother, if no one else, has a right to know you're getting married."

"I don't need my momma's permission to get married!" Leon retorted, "Or anyone else's."

"Dale's, you mean," Cutter replied softly.

"Dale's got no hold on me," Leon said with telling blandness.

"But he doesn't exactly see it that way," Cutter said. "As far as he's concerned you're his baby brother and it's his job to keep you from doing anything—"

"That *he* wouldn't do," Leon finished for him, and this time she could hear his exasperation. "But that's just it, I am not my brother. I'm my own man, and I do things in my own way, including getting married. So it doesn't make a damned bit of difference what Dale thinks or says about this, Cutter, not for my sake, anyway."

"Cassie," was the instant reply.

"Cassie," confirmed Leon. "You think I want him ripping up at her? And you know what he'd think and say about all this. I'd be putting my fist in his face, Cutter, and that'd do my momma a lot of good, now wouldn't it?"

"It's going to come sooner or later, man," Cutter warned him gently.

"Later then," Leon said gruffly, and his angrily clumping footsteps told Cassie he was coming closer.

She hopped back to the center of the room and folded her hands demurely. He took one look at her and the frown on his face upended itself. An almost giddy warmth suffused her, a certainty of the heart. All right, maybe his brother wouldn't like her. Maybe Leon's whole family would be aghast to find him married to a woman whom he'd met through an advertisement, and maybe the two of them hadn't been completely honest with one another, but that didn't mean they shouldn't be together. Whatever her other mistakes, marrying this man was the right thing to do. She knew it instinctively, no matter what anyone else might say, his brother Dale included. She extended a hand to him, and it was precisely then that the doorbell rang. Suddenly Dolores swept through the room in a cloud of spicy perfume and an instant later led the bemused minister to them.

Before Cassie knew what was happening to her, she was standing at Leon's side, clutching a bouquet in one hand—courtesy of the Pattersons—and feeling Leon slip a ring onto the other. And then it was done. She looked up into his shining eyes and heard him whisper, "That's it then. You and me together, girl, always," and she tilted her head back to welcome the kiss that sealed it. She knew, had to trust, in that moment that any problems would work themselves out. She just couldn't believe anything else. She couldn't.

Leon hustled her out of there with what he knew was indecent haste, rebuffing Dolores's offers of champagne toasts and wedding suppers as good-naturedly as he could. It was Cutter who finally restrained his wife, however, coming up behind her to clamp one hand down on her shoulder and the other over her mouth. "We'll see you folks later," he said with a wink. Leon grinned and tipped his hat, pushing Cassie through the open door with a hand in the small of her back.

"That was rude!" Cassie said, her smile and the sparkle of her eyes removing any sting from the words.

"You want to go back in?" he asked, wanting to eat her alive. She smiled and shook her head. "Come on, then." He took her hand and led her to the truck, letting her in on the driver's side. She slid beneath the steering wheel to the center of the seat but no farther. He folded himself in beside her and lifted his arm about her shoulders, kissing her long and heatedly. "Lord, this waiting's been killing me," he said against her temple.

"Me, too," she whispered, laying her hand upon his thigh. He trembled just at the weight of it, slight as it was. "But you were right," she told him. "This way is best. Thank you."

He felt like the biggest man in the world then, knowing that no one could argue with what he'd done and how he'd done it. Well, maybe one person could. Dale could argue with a fence post. But he didn't want to think about Dale or anyone but his new wife. Wife. Cripes. He was a married man. He marveled at that as he drove to the motel. Once there, he had to restrain himself from leaping from the truck. He took his time, moving as slowly as he could make himself do, manipulating the gear shift into place, killing the engine, extracting the keys, smiling in a way that he hoped would not betray either his eagerness or his nervousness. She surprised him with her calm.

"Aren't we going in?"

"Sure."

"Well?" He could only look at her, amazed and pleased. She actually laughed. "So move it, cowboy. You have an anxious bride on your hands."

He practically did leap from the truck then, hauling her out with him and pulling her up the stairs two at a time. When he got the door opened, however, he paused and turned to face her. "I suppose I really ought to do this when we get home," he said, momentarily distracted by the dreamy look that slackened her face.

"Home," she echoed, the word warming him as it never had before.

"Welcome, Mrs. Paradise," he said, scooping her up into his arms.

She looped her arms about his neck. "Thank you, Mr. Paradise," she said softly. "Now will you please make love to me?"

His heart bounced off the walls of his chest. "Darlin', you don't have to ask me twice!" he said, stepping through the door and shouldering it closed. His arm holding her against his chest, he dropped her legs, but instead of reaching toward the floor, she wrapped them around his waist, her skirt gaping wide and showing creamy thighs bare of stockings.

"I'm so proud," she said, "and so happy and so—"

Whatever else she might have said he forestalled with his mouth on hers as he carried her to the bed. Then it was too late for words, too late for anything except making her his in the way that mattered most, his and only his. Maybe he wasn't her first husband, but he was her only husband, and somehow that was more important, especially as she so obviously welcomed him and made him hers. Only hers.

They phoned for pizza about ten o'clock, ate in bed, and made love again afterward, laughing as they kissed away the smears of tomato sauce and melted cheese. It was late when they woke the next morning, and far later still when they managed to get their clothes back on again and went out for lunch. Sophía fed them on the house when she heard the news, squawking like a mother hen and claiming credit for the whole romance. It was to her as though Cassie had dropped out of the sky right at her feet and she had thrust her into Leon's empty arms.

"Oh, you're a man's best friend," Leon told her, feeding the illusion. "Maybe you ought to go into business as a matchmaker, Soph. I'd sure write you a glowing recommendation." He said the last with a wink at Cassie. She beamed at him, happier than she could quite believe.

Afterward, he showed her around town, what there was of it, and pointed out the various mountain ranges that surrounded them, telling her that one day soon he'd take her to see the MacDonald Observatory and Ft. Davis to the southeast and the Guadalupes to the north. To the northwest lay Carlsbad Caverns, and then there was El Paso and Mexico, and he remembered a lovely little Bed and Breakfast in Marfa that they ought to visit sometime on their way to Big Bend. After the grand tour, they went back to the motel, where they shared a long, hot kiss, after which he surprised her once again by declaring that later she should put on that white miniskirt he'd bought her and come dancing with him. "I've got a hankering to kick up my heels and show you off a little," he said, walking her toward the bed. "Later." Much later, as it turned out.

The club was right there in the motel and featured a band with a Latin-flavored country sound. It proved to be a popular local Saturday night watering hole. They got there late, drawing attention the moment they walked through the door. It was the Pattersons who greeted them first, but in no time at all they were surrounded by other friends of Leon's. The news was out. Leon introduced Cassie as "my little bride," and the Pattersons quickly repeated the details for anyone who hadn't already heard. They all moved to a table, and the new husband and wife took some good-natured ribbing about mail-order brides and such, but as one young lady put it, it was hard to argue with success.

"You're so obviously in love," she stated, making Cassie blush.

"Or heat," put in her husband, watching Leon nuzzle Cassie's ear. Everyone laughed, but someone else wisely submitted that it took some of both.

"Staying in love and in heat is the only way I know of to make it work," he said. Sounds of agreement went around the table, but Leon merely winked at Cassie, his grin seeming to say that they had everything they needed. She gripped his hand under the table, almost painfully happy, and tried to tell him with her eyes how deeply she cared for him.

Dancing with Leon was sheer heaven. They'd had enough practice to move well together, but never before had their dancing been imbued with such emotion. It was the same steps, of course, even the same music, but every touch now called to mind the loving they had shared and woke fresh desires and deepening needs for more of the same. It was a splendid agony, purposefully prolonged so that the pleasure would be more intense, and Leon did more than his fair share of stoking the fire.

"You are one hot-looking cowgirl in that outfit, Mrs. Paradise," he told her as they danced close. "I can hardly wait to get you out of it."

More than once he covertly slid his hands over parts of her body best touched only in private, and he not only kept kissing her everywhere, her shoulders, her chin, her hands, her ears, her nose and so on, but he also kept plucking at the top of the elastic tube she wore under her jacket. It would have been downright embarrassing if he hadn't been so adroit at picking his moments. As it was, by the time the party broke up, he had her wound up so tight that she could barely keep her hands to herself. She didn't, in fact, manage to do so before they got back to their room, so that they wound up kissing and touching one another down a long hallway, up a flight of stairs and along a landing. They were lip-locked when Leon finally managed to get the key in the hole. They were tearing at each other's clothes when the door crashed open and they tumbled inside. "I love you!" she whispered, uncertain if he even heard her as he scooped her up and carried her to bed. She didn't have time to think about that—or the desire, and by the time she could have, sleep was already overtaking her.

They were absolutely decadent and had breakfast in bed the next morning, though Leon had to first throw on his jeans and go out for cinnamon rolls, coffee and a cola. Leon seemed perfectly fine though he'd had a few beers the night before. Cassie hugged to herself the knowledge that this man of hers was no drinker. She would have sooner starved in the street than marry herself to a hard drinking man like her father. Leon had seemed hardly to notice that the alcohol was available. He had seemed high and loose on the congratulations of his friends and the good feelings between the two of them. She was high on him, and she never wanted to come down to earth.

That afternoon as they drove out to the ranch, Leon apologized for the lack of a "real" honeymoon, but she laughed and told him truthfully that just being with him was honeymoon enough for her. Besides, they had all the privacy they could want for now.

"But I have work to do, sugar," he told her. "I'd spend my days with you if I could, but a place like ours takes constant looking after."

A place like ours. Her smile was tremulous, laden with emotion. As easy as that he'd given her everything for which he'd worked so hard. Everything she and Jos had had—and God knew it had been little enough—they had acquired together. It amazed her that Leon could have worked so hard for so long and accomplished so very much alone and still be so very willing to share, so very generous, so very loving. She wound her arm about his neck and laid her head upon his shoulder. "That's all right. We'll have the nights."

"Yes, ma'am," he promised, laying a big hand on her knee. "We'll always have the nights."

She laughed softly and caught his hand as it wandered up her thigh. "Besides, in case you haven't noticed—and being a man you wouldn't—I have plenty to do myself."

"I take it there's more to housework than I've realized," he said. "I guess you have some getting ready to do for the boy, too, don't you?"

"Umm."

"One thing, though, if you're not too busy," he said.

She lifted her head and looked at his strong profile. "What's that?"

He squirmed a little, readjusting his body beneath the steering wheel. "Just for this time we're alone," he said hesitantly, and she noted that his voice had taken on that husky, velvety timbre he used when he made love to her. She pressed herself against him, his upper arm hard against the soft weight of her breasts. "I won't be needing those cold showers," he said. "If you could find the time to heat us some water...."

Us. The two of them in that big old bathtub. Heat shimmered through her. His hand moved up her thigh again. She swallowed to clear her throat. "I can manage that," she said.

He flashed her a grin and slid his hand higher still. "Now *that's* my idea of a honeymoon."

She closed her eyes and let the vision envelop her. Apparently they had more in common than either of them had realized.

They were happy, so very happy, the kind of happy that produced contentment all around them. Cassie spent her days nesting—organizing cupboards, rearranging closets, putting up shelves. She washed windows and walls and floors, beat rugs and scrubbed them. When she asked Leon if she could paint the kitchen cabinets as well as the walls, he laughed and said she could paint anything she pleased. She could paint cactus, as far as he was concerned, so long as it made her happy. She retorted primly that she didn't think that would be necessary, but if it was, she'd let him know so he could move a few closer to the house. "I'd do it," he said with endearing sincerity, "provided you'd kiss all the places the needles stick me and make them better."

"I'd kiss anything you wanted me to," she said flippantly.

He grinned. "Well, in that case, darlin', get on over here. I'm pretty sure I can find something that needs kissing right now." It seemed he always could, but to say that she didn't mind was to understate the case badly. She was a woman in love, and those were glorious days and nights filled with much more than kissing.

Leon took the reordering of his home in good stride. He didn't care what she did to the place, he said, as long as it was still standing when he came in of an evening. So Cassie moved furniture and painted and carted anything that wasn't absolutely necessary out to one of the storage sheds. She was making as much room as possible, and Leon wasn't so besotted that he didn't notice. "I know the place is small," he said one evening after she'd asked him about the possibility of creating more closet space, "but I'm intending to build on before long. I'd like to put it off some, though, if you think we can hold out for a bit once young Pete comes. Seems to me it might be wiser to get a hold on that extra range first. Takes a lot to feed a cow out here, and every head of beef we can run is money in our pockets come spring. A family takes more upkeep than a single man, and it seems to me we ought to be thinking about that."

She put on a bright smile and told him that he was right, of course, but the time when she could bring her brothers to Texas was seeming further and further away rather than closer and closer. How long would Chintz tolerate them? Were they safe even now? Did they miss her? Did they go to sleep every night thinking that tomorrow would be the day she'd send for them? She told herself that she was being melodramatic, but she could not quite escape the feeling that a dark cloud was hovering high above her golden, happy world. She tried, though.

Dodie had called to say that arrangements had been made for Newt to bring Petey down on the bus at the end of the coming week, so it wouldn't be long now before she had the two of them with her. She intended to persuade Leon that Newt should stay. But that left Freddy, and Bart and Kyler and Kole on their on with Chintz and Marlene, and that worried her. The twins simply weren't strong enough to protect the youngest two. They were used to taking off whenever things got tricky, but that left Freddy and Barton to deal with Marlene's pettiness and Chintz's meanness on their own. She remembered Bart's broken glasses and bit her lip. How would he see if Chintz knocked them off his face again? What joke would Freddy be able to make if Marlene did him real physical harm?

But they would be all right somehow. She had to believe that the boys would be all right. Otherwise, the guilt she felt at being so happy while they remained in such a desperate situation would overwhelm her and perhaps even ruin her chances of bringing them here to live with her and Leon. She had to be sensible. She had to take it slowly, get Leon used to the idea gradually. Somehow she would convince him that they could all make it together, that the boys wouldn't be any real trouble. She didn't know how she was going to do that except by loving him to the very best of her ability and showing him how hard she would work to take the burdens of the household from him.

To that end, she had the house shining by the time the evening came to make the long drive into Van Horn to meet Petey and Newt. Leon had surprised her by providing a door for their bedroom. It was built from a store of lumber that he kept in the barn and mounted with huge triangular hinges meant for swinging far heavier objects. She had painted that, too, and thanked him for assuring their privacy.

"Well," he'd said, grinning at her, "I don't know about you, but as far as I'm concerned, the honeymoon's far from over."

She had taken a long time showing him just how she felt about continuing the honeymoon. It was only the need to be at the bus stop when Petey arrived that kept her from succumbing completely. He didn't press her, seeming to understand that she was anxious to see her son for the first time in nearly a month. If only he knew how she loved him for that, but she didn't tell him. Her desire to see her son again—and to speak to Newt privately before he said something he shouldn't to Leon—distracted her to the point that for once she didn't even reflect on how much easier it would be to tell her husband that she loved him if he would first tell her that his feelings went as deep.

They left in plenty of time, but unlike the night Cassie had arrived, the streets were not deserted. As soon as they entered town, a pickup truck passing in the opposite direction stopped, turned around and caught up with them, flashing its brights in an effort to pull them over. Leon identified it as belonging to one of the fellows they'd met at the dance the night after they'd married. He stuck his arm out the window and motioned for the truck to follow. When they pulled into a parking spot in front of Sofía's, the other truck was right behind them. The bus was pulling in, too—early.

"You go on and meet the boy," Leon said, leaning across her to open her door. "I'll have a word with this character and meet you in a minute. Give you a chance for a private hello."

Cassie smiled. Fate, it seemed, was going to be generous. This way, she might get in a few brief, well-chosen words of warning to Newt before Leon arrived. She leaned across the cab to place a kiss on his cleanly shaven cheek. He looked so handsome. She was proud to be at his side and anxious for Newt and Petey to meet him. She got out and hurried around the building. The bus driver had already opened the luggage compartment and was busy setting out half a dozen cardboard boxes. Apparently, Van Horn was the destination of several travelers this evening. She didn't have time to ponder the matter, however, as Newt was even then stepping down from the idling bus, a sleeping Petey cradled in his arms. They were here! She rushed forward, eager to embrace them. Then someone else stepped down, someone she couldn't help recognizing even though his hair was standing at odd angles and his glasses were missing.

"Barton?" she said aloud, not daring to believe her own eyes.

He squinted in her direction, a smile on his face, but before she could digest this shock, she got another, three of them actually, as the twins clambered to the ground, dragging a groggy Freddy, each with a hold under one arm.

"Cass!" someone shouted, and was instantly hushed by Newt hissing, "Quiet, dipstick! Want to wake the baby?"

He turned toward her and smiled apologetically. "Hi, sis. Surprise."

Surprise? *Surprise?* She put her hands to her head, thrilled to the core to see every one of the scamps and utterly, desperately horrified. Her brain formed just one thought, *All six! All six!* But none of the awful implications were lost to her. She knew—oh, God, how she knew—that her wonderful little world was about to take a sharp swerve into a universe of hurt feelings and suspicion, and the worst part was that Leon's suspicions would be true. She had used him, and she had intended to use him from the very beginning. She just hadn't intended to fall in love with him! She had thought vaguely in terms of a bargain, shelter and support for herself and the boys in return for housekeeping, companionship and, yes, even sex. But that idea had dissolved somewhere along the line. After she'd met him, after she'd come to know him... Oh, God, would he understand how much she loved him? Why hadn't she told him how much she loved him?

She dropped both hands, suddenly too weak to hold them up any longer. Newt walked toward her, Petey rousing enough to partially sit up and cling to his uncle's neck. He turned his head as they drew near, smiled and reached out for her. "Mama," he said, his little boy's voice husky with sleep.

Love flooded her, love for her son and her brothers and her husband, and the tears started. "Oh, Petey!" she cried, grabbing him to her. He wrapped his legs around her waist and laid his head on her shoulder. He was so heavy! He had grown, and she hadn't been there to see it, but she couldn't think of that now. She couldn't seem to think at all. Newt stepped close.

"It's all right, isn't it, Cassie? It's what we planned, to live out here together. Besides, we didn't know what else to do. Pa said they couldn't stay with him anymore, and Dodie didn't have room for them. She called the girls and they all scraped together the money. Denise and Fayrene said to say thanks for them, and Margie just said she was sorry she couldn't give no more than twenty bucks. There wasn't time to call again, and Dodie said it was probably better anyhow, as she couldn't think of nothing else to do. I figured she was right since you got him to marry you like you said you'd do. She put in a bunch of the money herself. Said not to tell you, but I figured you had ought to know. Anyway, it'll be all right, won't it?"

"All right?" she echoed. Something pierced the fog of her emotions just then, a sense of someone's presence. Leon. She whirled around, Petey all over her. He was standing at the corner of the building, his thumbs hooked in his pockets, his mouth slightly ajar, a look of shock on his face.

"Cass?" Newt said again. The sound of his voice, the dread of what he might say, what would have to be said, made her whirl back to face him. "It's all right, isn't it?" he went on. "You got him to marry you just like you—"

"Newt!" She didn't know what else to say or do. She could feel Leon at her back, sizing things up, figuring things out, not that much was left to his imagination once Kole stepped forward.

"What's the big deal?" he asked grumpily. "She promised we could live with them, didn't she? You always said she promised."

Newt's eyes had gone from Cassie to Leon and back again, and his brow was furrowed with worry. He turned on Kole almost savagely. "Shut up, and stay shut up! Cassie and me'll take care of everything. Won't we, Cassie?" That last was plaintive, boyish, frightened.

Cassie gulped. "Yes. Oh!" Instinctively, mechanically, she muddled through. "What a nice surprise! But...you should have called first. We...we aren't set up yet for...company."

Newt bowed his head, and she heard him whisper, "Sorry."

Tears were rolling down her face. She felt them when she forced her smile, her heart squeezing. Newt looked so forlorn. All of them, they looked so lost, and she had promised. She had promised to take care of them. She closed her eyes briefly, hoping bitterly that Leon would understand, knowing he wouldn't. But whatever happened, she had promised. They were her brothers. She held Petey with one arm tucked under his bottom and spread the other arm in welcome. "I'm so glad to see you all," she said, and suddenly they swamped her, Barton first, his face shining, then the twins and Newt.

Freddy hung back, alternately rubbing his eyes with his fists and looking around him. Apparently, he'd spotted the tall cowboy at the corner of the building and decided to try his luck there. Cassie watched from a web of hugging arms as he walked toward Leon, dragging his toes in the dust. He stopped in front of him and tilted his head far back. "Hi," he said. "I'm Freddy."

A muscle worked in the hollow of Leon's jaw. "One of the brothers," he deduced tightly.

Freddy had seen danger often enough to recognize it now. He turned a look at Cassie. "I must be tired," he said on a sigh. "I can't think of anything funny."

"Oh, I don't know," Leon drawled, his gaze holding his wife's. "Doesn't everybody always laugh when someone else is made out a chump?"

"It isn't like that!" she gasped, but he just turned around and walked away. She closed her eyes, lips trembling, and vowed that she would make him understand. Somehow, some way, she would make him see that she loved him and that they could make this work. Somehow. Oh, please, God. Somehow.

Chapter Six

Cassie watched as they clustered in the middle of the small room and looked the place over, their arms full of boxes and bundles and dirty sweaters. Petey had his fingers in his mouth, his hair in his face, and a shoe in the crook of one arm. His little eyes were so sleepy that she doubted he could actually see anything at all. It would have been a poignant moment full of tender, motherly love if not for the angry cowboy seething at her back. He had primed and started the generator before they'd left the house that afternoon, assuring them this electric light that filled the place. She had the feeling he regretted it. She had the feeling he regretted everything that had anything to do with her. It was a feeling she couldn't bear.

Desperately, she moved into the middle of the group, smoothing hair and patting shoulders. Barton discovered the chair and plopped himself into it, testing it with light bounces of his wiggling rump. He alone could not take the measure of this new home. Cassie ran a finger along the line of his brows.

"What happened to your glasses?" she whispered.

He shrugged, too eager to see what the others could to make a coherent answer. "Somewheres," was all he said.

Newt made a sound of disgust. "It was that Marlene," he declared. "It had to be! He never went anywhere without his glasses, even wore 'em to bed, you know he did! Then he woke up one morning and they's gone. Marlene said he couldn't go to school without them, and Pa said we couldn't afford another pair, that he'd have to go down to Welfare to get 'em, but I wouldn't let him go. I was afraid they'd take him away and just when you were getting everything together for us here in Texas!"

Cassie drew a sharp breath, and Newt sent an apologetic glance at Leon, who rested both forearms in the doorway, his feet planted firmly on the porch. His eyes, full of accusation, never left her, and he never said a word, but his silence was more malignant than anything he might have voiced. Trembling, she brushed at Bart's golden brown hair and did automatically what she'd always done, tried to reassure. "It'll be all right," she said softly. "School doesn't start for weeks and weeks yet. We'll get them replaced before then." Somehow. "I promise." Another promise she would have to find a way to keep. It felt enormous, as if a huge boulder had dropped onto her shoulders, but she would find a way. Somehow. She dared not think how just yet. Bart, too, wanted to move on to other things.

"So what's it like?" he asked eagerly.

Everyone knew that he was asking about the house.

"Small," one of the twins said, looking around.

"It's big enough," Newt hastily corrected.

"It's square," Freddy said, "and *flat.*"

The others laughed, all but Leon, who said and did nothing, only stared at her as if she might change shape before his very eyes. She tried her best to ignore him. Silent pleading had done no good, so why not? She turned her attention to the impish face looking up at her.

"It's not that it's *flat,* Freddy," she said indulgently. "The house is made of adobe brick, and it's dry out here, so things don't warp and swell up like they did back in the hills, that's all."

"Oh." He seemed to look around him with new appreciation, but he was just being Freddy in truest form. "Does that mean all the girls are flat-chested?" he quipped shrewdly. Cassie's mouth dropped open. The twins and Barton sniggered behind their hands. Only Newt flashed an uncomfortable look at Leon and scolded.

"Cut it out, Fred!"

Freddy lifted his eyebrows and gave Newt the most patently innocent look imaginable. Cassie changed the subject. "There are two bedrooms," she said loudly.

Kole opened the newly constructed door and stuck his head inside. "This one's pretty big," he announced.

Kyler performed a similar inspection behind the curtain draping the other doorway. "This one's not much bigger than the bed."

"Why aren't there any windows in here?" Freddy queried, looking pointedly at the east wall.

"It's to help it stay cool in the daytime," Cassie answered. "That's why the walls are so thick, too."

"There's a window in here," Kyler said, still inspecting the small bedroom.

"Here, too," Kole put in.

"That's so the morning sun can wake you," Cassie said, parroting explanations given her by Leon in the early days, easy days. She sneaked a glance at Leon, saw a new accusation in those glaring eyes, and mentally jerked away. "Th-there's a bathroom, too, with running water and everything, no hot, but the toilet flushes, a-and there's a real washing machine on the back porch. I-It's hooked up to a battery with a solar panel." This news was greeted with gasps of wonder. "Oh, and the kitchen floor's wood because there's a cold cellar beneath it."

"What's that?" Bart wanted to know, face screwed up as he tried to imagine such a thing.

"Well," Cassie explained, "back in the hills we had a smoke house for curing and storing our meats and such. A cold cellar's kind of like that. It's a room dug down into the earth where it's cool and dark. We keep our perishables down there. That way we don't need a refrigerator, so we don't have to run the electric generator during the day. There's a door that lifts up right out of the floor and a stairway down to it, and there's another one on the west side of the house. A long time ago that would've been an escape route in case of an Indian attack. Isn't that smart?"

Bart shrugged, but Freddy was intrigued. "Was there really Indian attacks?" he asked eagerly. Petey perked up enough to make whoops and stomp around like an Indian dancing.

It was a story she hoped Leon might tell. "W-We'll talk about that another time," she said, aided by Newt, who had let curiosity overcome concern and peeked into the kitchen.

"Hey, we got a phone!" he exclaimed, causing a stampede. Even Bart, who couldn't see, went to have a look. Petey, smallest and slowest, wormed and shoved his way through the legs of the others until he could get a look, too.

"Well, I declare," Kole said softly.

"What's it do?" Petey wanted to know.

"It lets you talk to people in other places, silly," Newt told him.

Freddy sighed and backed out of the doorway, shouldering his way past Kyler and Bart. "Too bad we ain't got nobody to call," he complained.

"We could call Dodie," Kyler suggested hopefully, "let her know we got here all right."

Newt rounded on him angrily. "Don't be so awful stupid!" he cried. "It costs money to make calls like that!"

"We're not calling anybody," she said. "Dodie won't be expecting a call, so she won't worry. I'll write her a letter. Now I don't want to hear any more about it."

"But Cassie...." Kole whined. It was then that Leon finally stepped into the house.

"It's time y'all were getting to bed," he said, his voice both deeper and sterner than usual. Petey uncorked his fingers from his mouth and stared with as much shock as if the couch had spoken.

Cassie was suddenly frightened, terrified. She didn't deserve a man like Leon. She didn't deserve him, and now she was going to lose him. Knowing what he knew, he couldn't want to keep her with him now. What that meant for the boys she couldn't bear to contemplate. She wanted to look to the doorway, but knowing what she'd see there kept her from it. She was trembling so badly she had to fold her arms around herself to still it.

Get through it, Cassie thought. *Just get through it.* She started appointing sleeping places. "Let's... Let's see. We'll make a pallet on the kitchen floor for N-Newt. The t-twins can have the small bedroom, and the c-couch'll fold down for Freddy and Bart. That leaves...."

"The boy can sleep with you," Leon said curtly.

She knew what that meant. Cold swept through her like a cutting winter wind. If they didn't sleep together, she and Leon, she'd have no way, no chance, to convince him to keep her. The sex, the *lovemaking,* was the one thing he couldn't deny, the one thing she couldn't possibly have faked. He had to know that. She had to make him believe that. She turned to him, but she couldn't quite meet his eyes with hers. "Don't be silly," she said, trying for a light tone that merely made her teeth click together. "He can sleep with Newt o-or with Freddy and Bart. Yes, that couch bed is big enough for three, a-and they're used to sleeping close, aren't you, boys? A-Anyway, where would you...." It was the wrong thing to say. She mustn't openly even entertain the idea that he might have meant to sleep elsewhere. "Our

PLAY

SILHOUETTE'S

HEARTS

GAME

AND YOU GET

- FREE BOOKS
- A FREE GIFT
- AND MUCH MORE

TURN THE PAGE AND DEAL YOURSELF IN

PLAY "LUCKY F
AND GET . . .

★ Exciting Silhouette Romance

★ "Key to Your Heart" Pendan

THEN CONTINUI
LUCKY STREAK Y
SWEETHEART OI

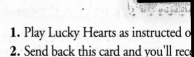

1. Play Lucky Hearts as instructed o

2. Send back this card and you'll rece
   Romance™ novels. These books h
   each, but they are yours to keep at

3. There's no catch. You're under no
   anything. We charge nothing—2
   shipment. And you don't have to
   number of purchases—not even

4. The fact is thousands of readers en
   mail from the Silhouette Reader Se
   convenience of home delivery...the
   novels months before they're availa
   our discount prices!

5. We hope that after receiving you
   remain a subscriber. But the cho
   or cancel, anytime at all! So why
   invitation, with no risk of any ki

ween his knees and leaned back against him, gazing up a
e stars. She thought about dancing with him in the dark
nd about long, lazy kisses and hands that had slid up her
des to skim her breasts, and she knew that he could have
oaxed her right into his bed at most any time. She swal-
owed and nodded. "Yes, I suppose I would have."

His fawn brown eyes flashed yellow with fire. "You'd do
nything for those boys, wouldn't you? Anything at all."

She didn't have to think about that one, though some-
hing told her she was damning herself. "Anything I had
o," she admitted, hurrying to add, "You don't know how
ad it was for them back at Pa's. I could protect them some
efore Marlene came, but after she married Pa it was just
opeless. Marlene didn't want them around, and whatever
Marlene wanted Marlene got, not that Pa ever cared about
e boys one way or another particularly, but Marlene did,
d she made their lives miserable. You heard what they
d she did to Bart's glasses! She stole them to make trou-
, to try to get him sent down to Welfare, so they'd take
n away. That's what would have happened, you know,
hout me there the Welfare folks would've taken them
y."

Well, maybe they should have," Leon muttered, rais-
her ire for the first time.

How can you say that?" she demanded. "You've got a
brother. How'd you like it if someone else decided to
im away."

y little brother's nearly as old as you!" Leon re-

hat's that got to do with anything? Suppose he was
age, or Freddy's?"

folks took care of him when he needed taking care

, mine didn't!" she said. "Ma did, but Pa
, so it was left to me, and I didn't know what else
had to get them away and make them a home
!"

---

bed," she said deliberately, "is for us," and to add believ-
ability, normalcy, she smiled and calmly lifted her gaze.

He just stood there, arms at his sides as if he'd forgotten
he had them. Only his eyes seemed animated. They were
flashing, popping, with a dozen emotions. Then he closed
them and took a deep breath, and when he opened them
again, there was nothing there, nothing at all. She reeled as
if he'd slapped her.

"Leon?"

He turned around and walked out. He didn't hurry. He
didn't jerk. He just shifted his feet and turned his body and
left. She watched him go out, heard the screen door squeak
and thump as it swung closed, and then she was staring at
nothing. She listened to the sounds of his footsteps as he
crossed the porch, then that, too, became nothing as he
stepped off onto the sand. He was leaving her, them. She
expected to hear the sound of the truck engine firing up any
moment. Horrified, terrorized, she ran after him, the screen
slamming behind her. She scanned the darkness, finding the
truck. He wasn't there. Movement caught at her sight from
the corner of her eye, and she turned in that direction. He
was walking toward the barn.

She slumped with relief. He wasn't leaving. Yes, he was.
He wasn't leaving the ranch, but he was leaving her, and she
couldn't let him do that. She couldn't. She started running
again. He heard her coming. He had to hear her coming.
Her footsteps were as loud in her ears as the slamming of
her heart. But if he heard, he gave no sign of it. He just
kept walking like a man with somewhere to go—or something to leave behind. She drew up close and stopped.

"Leon."

Nothing.

"Leon!"

He reached the barn and went inside, sliding the door
open and closed again behind him. She went after him,
afraid not to. She shoved the door open far enough to slip
inside. He was standing in the middle of the cement floor.

It was as clean as her mother's kitchen. That always amazed her, how clean and organized he kept everything in here. His back was to her, his hands at his hips, head bowed.

"Leon," she whispered, "please—"

"Don't!" he said, the word strangled and mangled. "Don't even try!" He put his head back. "Why waste the effort? I couldn't believe it anyway, now could I?"

She bit her lip, tears filling her eyes. "I didn't lie to you," she whispered. "I just didn't . . . tell you everything."

He laughed, but he didn't sound amused. "No, ma'am," he said, pushing his hat back on his head, "you sure didn't. Seems you left out a *lot*." He cocked his head as if mentally counting all the facts she'd never bothered to relate in her lifetime. "Let's see, there's Newt. Oh, you *mentioned* him, all right, but I don't remember hearing anything about him expecting to *live* with us. Then again, you didn't even let on there might be others. How many are there, anyway, Cassie?" He rounded on her and started ticking them off on his fingers. "Newt and Bart and Freddy and, of course, the twins, that's five. Did I forget anyone? Oh, Pete. The *one* I did know I'd be providing for, but, hey, what's five more? Right? If I'd take on one, why it just stands to reason I'd take on *six,* doesn't it?" He was shouting now, letting her have it with both barrels. "What were you going to do, Cassie? Sneak them in one at a time? Have all of them out for little visits that never ended? Didn't you think I'd notice?"

She didn't say anything, because what could she say? He didn't want or expect an answer anyway.

"That's what you've been doing all this time, making space for them! Isn't it? You weren't making *us* a home! You were making *them* a home!"

"Leon," she whispered pleadingly, "they're my brothers."

"And you promised them a place, didn't you? Well, didn't you, Cassie?"

She bowed her head. "Yes."

"You came to Texas for that very reason, didn'[...]

She didn't say anything. She didn't have to.

"You lying, cheating, lousy little . . . fraud," h[...] out. "You're not who I thought you were, Cassie[...] not *what* I thought you were. There's a word for[...] who use sex and lies to get what they want, Cassie,[...] my momma would slap me if I said it in her presen[...] it fits you, damnit!" But he didn't say it, and s[...] grateful for that much as she blinked back the tear[...]

He was silent after that for a long time, so long [...] began to climb up out of the hurt he'd heaped or[...] her. She thought of all the things she had to say, [...] bucked up her courage.

"I'm sorry, Leon," she began. "I should've [...] right up front, but I was scared you wouldn't [...] chance if I did."

"So you said nothing!" he accused.

"I was afraid," she reiterated.

"Afraid you'd lose your meal ticket."

"Afraid you wouldn't give me, us, a chance[...]

"Tell me something, Cassie," he said harsh[...] the day we went for the license, you'd have [...] then, wouldn't you?"

She knew the answer to that question w[...] tant to him, but she didn't know exactl[...] through with dishonesty, though, so it di[...] She lifted her gaze resolutely. "Yes."

"Even before that, if I'd pressed it, y[...] me then, too, wouldn't you?"

She thought about that, about how [...] made her shiver with longing somet[...] and male he'd looked when he'd c[...] shower beneath the windmill after [...] hair plastered back, dark with wate[...] fine arrow of hair. She thought a[...] kissed her after her bath, abou[...]

"So you married me!" he roared. "You'd do anything for them, *anything,* even marry me, even *sleep with me,* even *pretend* to—"

"I never pretended!" she cried.

"Never?" he demanded, advancing a step.

She held her ground and shook her head, whispering, "Never."

He stared at her a long, hard minute, and then he jerked his eyes away. "I don't believe you."

She felt as if the ground dropped away beneath her. "But you have to believe me," she said in a small voice.

"Have to?" He shook his head. "No. I *can't* believe you. You used me, Cassie. You let me think you cared."

"I do care! Leon, I love you."

"Oh, right. You came out here looking for a love match."

She gulped. "Not exactly."

"Not at all is more like it," he snapped. "God in heaven, Cassie, you were planning this all along, weren't you? From the moment you spotted my ad in that magazine."

"No! I swear it. I didn't even see the ad, you know that. Dodie saw it, and she told me about it, but I figured you were some nut with long hair and chin whiskers, a hermit, maybe. She's the one who wrote to you first. It was only after you wrote her back that I started thinking you might not be some wild man living in another century."

"But you figured I might be desperate enough to take on half a dozen boys," he prodded.

"No! The boys didn't come into it at all back then. You just seemed like a nice person. You had a way with words. I liked that, so I thought we'd correspond, that's all."

"You didn't think then about coming to Texas?"

It seemed an odd question, but she answered it as forthrightly as the others. "Of course not. How would I have gotten here? I sure didn't have the money to come on my own, and you hadn't invited me yet."

"But when I did you jumped at the chance, didn't you?"

"You know I didn't, not at first, but I thought I knew you by then, enough to think maybe we had a chance."

"And Chintz was making life miserable for all of you because Marlene wanted you out of the house, isn't that right?"

She took a series of shallow breaths, afraid but uncertain where the danger lay. "Pa was always making life miserable," she said carefully and licked her lips, "but it so happens that right after you invited me down here, he told me... well, he put us out, me and Petey."

"And the boys?"

She took a deep breath. "He... He didn't threaten to put them out exactly, but he...." She licked her lips again and swallowed. "He said that Marlene wanted to live like they were a *normal* married couple, like their baby, *their* family was all there was."

"Meaning he didn't want them," Leon said dully.

"Meaning he didn't want them," she echoed sadly.

He brought his hands to his hips again, then abruptly threw them up into the air. "And here sat dumb old Leon," he said, "down here on twenty thousand acres of Texas all by his lonesome, plump for the picking!"

She squeezed her eyes shut and capitulated. "All right! That's exactly what I thought at first. I came determined to make you marry me so I'd have a place to bring the boys! But after I met you... Well, you were so much more than I expected, not at all the sort of man you'd figure would advertise for a wife." He snorted at that, but she hurried on. "I saw how it was right away. You're a fine man, a man any woman would be proud to have for a husband, but you just hadn't found anyone you wanted yet. Living out here all alone like that, you didn't have a chance to meet any new women, and you obviously hadn't found the right one back in town. I just wanted a chance with you, Leon, is that so bad? I just wanted a chance... and then I wanted *you*."

His face was utterly implacable. Silence descended while he stared, and then he struck a cryptic pose, one knee bent, head cocked, arms folded. "What you mean is that then you saw that *I* wanted *you,* only you couldn't be sure how badly I wanted you because I didn't drag you right off to bed. Oh, no! Not me. I was too stupid to know I could've had you at any moment!"

"That's not true!"

"Isn't it? Didn't you say a minute ago that you'd have slept with me even before I asked you to marry me?"

She gulped. "I didn't mean it like that. I meant I was attracted to you right from—"

"I could be fat, bald, and over the hill and you'd be saying the same thing!"

"I wouldn't! I'd have laid it all out with you. I'd have struck a bargain!"

"Why didn't you tell me then?" he demanded. "Why didn't you just tell me about the rest of them when you told me about Pete?"

She grabbed the hair at her temples in frustration. "I was afraid!"

"Afraid I didn't want you badly enough to overlook a little thing like five extra mouths to feed!"

"Yes!" she screamed. "I was afraid you didn't want me badly enough!"

"Well, I did," he said quietly. "I wanted you so badly I was afraid of mucking it up. I wanted to do it right with you, Cassie. That's why I waited!"

"So did I! That's exactly how I felt!"

"Only you weren't looking for love with me, Cassie," he said. "You were looking for a meal ticket for six boys, and it could've been Satan himself, but you'd still have married him."

"But it was you, Leon," she told him, tears spilling from her eyes. "It was you!"

"That's right, it was me!" he said bitterly. "Maybe you didn't come looking for love, Cassie, but I *did,* and that was the problem."

"No. It wasn't. I mean, all right, I didn't come looking for love, but—"

"You found what you were looking for, Cassie," he said flatly. "You found a sap with stars in his eyes. And I found a fake."

"No!"

"No? Then why didn't you tell me?"

I was afraid! she wanted to scream, but what good would that do? She'd tried to explain that already. She didn't know what else to say, how to convince him that what they had was real. If only she could hold him, touch him, ignite that passion that always sparked between them. But when she stepped forward, he jerked back.

"Leave me alone, Cassie, just leave me alone," he said tiredly.

There were shadows around his eyes, and his shoulders slumped. He looked for all the world as if he could sleep standing on his feet. Maybe a night's sleep would do them both some good.

"Where'll you stay?" she asked softly.

He jerked his head. "Here."

"In the barn?"

"I've slept in worse."

"Leon, just come on into the house, please!"

He shook his head. "House isn't big enough for all of us."

"That doesn't matter. We can manage."

"I don't want to manage, Cassie," he said. "I just want to be left alone."

"Leon," she whispered, *"please!"*

He turned his back on her. She stood for a time, wringing her hands and trying to form an effective appeal, but all the words had been said, and the damage had been done, and she couldn't take any of it back or start over again. In the end, she did as he'd asked and left him alone.

When she stepped up onto the porch, Newt stepped out of the shadows. "Cassie," he whispered, "ain't he coming in?"

She shook her head and wiped surreptitiously at tears. Newt sighed.

"We screwed things up for you, didn't we?"

She tried to put a good face on it. "It'll be all right."

He slid an arm around her shoulders. "I'm sorry, sis. I just didn't know what else to do."

She patted his head, realizing as she did just how far she had to reach up to do it. "It'll work out."

"I hope so. He wasn't expecting us, was he? I mean, he didn't know, did he?"

She shook her head sorrowfully, and suddenly she couldn't hold back anymore. She turned her face into his bony chest and wept. "It's all my fault! I couldn't tell him, Newt. I wanted to, but I just couldn't tell him. I was afraid to tell him."

He pushed her back, his hands at her shoulders, and she realized in that moment just how much of a man he was now. "You scared of him?" he demanded in a harsh whisper. "He hurt you?"

"No!" She shook her head, sniffing. "It's not like that. Leon's not like Pa. He'd never *hit* me. It's just... Oh, it's so messed up, Newt. If only I'd told him about the other boys! I see now I should've told him! But I was so afraid he wouldn't believe that it was *him* I wanted. But he doesn't believe it now anyway, so what does it matter?"

Newt dropped his hands to his sides and shifted his weight. "Cassie, you're not making a lot of sense here," he said in the very same voice he'd have used to tell Kole to shut up or Kyler to stop it. That made her smile and the tears to start pouring down her face again.

"I can't help it," she whispered. "He's wonderful, Newt, as wonderful as Jos, in his own way."

Newt whistled softly. "You're some set up on him then, huh?"

She had to laugh. "You could say that."

"Well, what's the problem then?" Newt reasoned. "He'll come around, won't he? Jos would have."

"Maybe," she said. "Maybe Jos would have, but Jos knew I loved him, Newt. He didn't have to wonder why I married him."

"'Course he didn't," Newt said matter-of-factly. "Ever'body knew you married him to get away from Pa."

Cassie gasped. "I did not!" But she had. Seemed she was always marrying somebody for the wrong reason, but it had worked out with Jos, and it could work out with Leon, if he'd let it. "Never you mind about that," she said to Newt. "You ought to be asleep."

He wrinkled his nose at that. "Floor's awful hard, Cass."

"Well, it'll have to do," she said. "We'll pile up some blankets."

"Couldn't find none extra."

"Towels, then," she said decisively. "Leon...*we* have some mighty good towels, if I do say so myself, and there's sleeping bags. That'll take care of it for tonight. Tomorrow I'll get one of the little boys to sleep on them, and you can have his place."

"I could sleep out here," he offered. "I wouldn't mind sleeping under the stars." He leaned against the porch post and gazed up into the heavens.

Cassie did likewise. "I know what you mean. It's something, isn't it, that sky? Leon told me about it in his letters, but you just have to see it to understand. It's like... forever...with diamonds."

"Forever with diamonds," he echoed. "Yeah. That's what it is, all right. Man, it's beautiful! Wish I could draw it, but there just isn't any way to put it on paper. It'd take paint or ink, maybe, but that's more than I know how to do."

"My artist," she said fondly. Then, on impulse, she slipped her arms around him and hugged him. "I'm glad you're here!"

He looped his arms loosely about her shoulders. "This place is right, Cass," he said. "I can feel it in my bones."

"I've thought so, too," she whispered. "If only...."

"I'm just sorry we caused so much trouble," he went on when she didn't, "all coming together this way."

"At least I know you're all safe," she said. *For now.* She closed her eyes, unwilling even to think about what they'd do or where they'd go if Leon put them out. "It'll work out," she said as much to herself as to the boy who was fast becoming a man. "It'll work out."

It had to. It just had to.

Chapter Seven

Leon threw the blanket over the stall gate and plopped down onto a nearby bale of hay. The pain was as physical as any he'd ever experienced. Had he sustained a genuine wound, he would have felt certain that he was dying. He wasn't entirely sure that he wouldn't, anyway, unless he pulled himself together. But how to do it?

She had lied to him. Whatever she said now, nothing could change that, and all they'd said that night after the boys had arrived was hard to overcome. The things he'd said to her! And she had just stood there and taken it, but what else could she do? He was right. She had lied and schemed and plotted, played him for the worst sort of fool. Nevertheless, try as he might, he could find no way out of this mess that was his marriage.

He could divorce her, certainly, maybe even get an annulment, but where would she go? What would she do? That was why, despite everything, he'd loaded everybody into the truck and brought them all back to the Paradise. What else could he do? She couldn't hope to support herself and six—God in heaven, six!—boys out here. Van Horn was a small town. Jobs were not plentiful, and those available did not pay much beyond minimum wage. It would be the same back in West Virginia, only worse, he suspected. Otherwise, she wouldn't have chosen this desperate path. He'd briefly contemplated driving her and the boys into El Paso and putting up a few months' rent for them. Her chances of finding work would be better there, but even then she was probably looking at minimum wage. Still, they could survive for a while, provided she could hold on to what she earned. Cassie, however, was a self-described "hill girl" unused to city ways. She'd be an easy mark for any smooth-talking, sweet-smiling hustler who came her way.

He told himself that she need not be his problem, that she didn't deserve his concern because she had clearly used him. But he could not find a way to wash his hands of her and those boys and live with his conscience, not yet, anyway. In time, he assured himself, he would find a way out. Meanwhile, he was sleeping in his barn, living as separate a life as he could manage from those in his house, and hurting.

He had believed she loved him. He had *wanted* to believe she loved him, and he might have gone on doing so if her brothers hadn't shown up all at once and spilled the beans. *"You got him to marry you, just like you said. You promised we could come live with you."* Those words rolled through his head over and over and over. *You got him to marry you... You got him to marry you...* He sighed, wishing he could go to sleep and wake up and find it was all a bad dream. *You promised... You promised... You promised...* "You promised to love and honor me," he said softly, and it ached. Oh, how it hurt to know it was all a lie.

She was so good, too! She had been so convincing. He tried not to think of the nights or the afternoons or the mornings they had spent in bed. He tried not to remember dancing close and laughing softly and working hard together. He didn't want to recall dinners by candlelight, making love in the bathtub, shivering together beneath a cold shower and afterward toweling each other off until the heat warmed them from within. Even this barn held certain bittersweet memories. Neither was he free from images of her riding out across the range alone on horseback. He had become so used to dreaming of her during the workday, of wanting to get back to her, of letting her soothe away the little irritations and stoke the fires that, briefly, had brightened his nights. In such a short time he had become so used to loving her that it did not seem he could stop, and more than anything else, he wanted to stop loving her. If only he could stop loving her, he could stop hurting. He could stop wanting what he couldn't have.

Not that she'd turned him out. She was willing to go on as before, or so she'd said. She had even said that she loved him, but how could he believe that now? At most, she might feel gratitude toward him for not leaving her and those kids standing in that dusty street, but gratitude was not what he wanted from her. Subservience and lip service and calculated passion were substitutes for what he wanted, poor indeed, and even she ought to be able to understand that. He simply could not live with false passion. He could not live with the kind of regret and recrimination he saw in her now. A guilty conscience was not the firmest foundation for a marriage, and yet he couldn't seem to let her go. Neither could he live with this pain, and yet somehow he did, but the effort that required was amazing. No matter how much sleep he managed to get, he woke exhausted and drained the next morning.

The barn door slid open. One of the boys. He could tell because they always slid the door all the way open, while Cassie opened a space just big enough to slip through. He sighed and whacked dust from his chaps, too tired to get up and look busy. Newt stuck his head around the corner of the stall.

"Hey, Mr. Paradise."

"Newt."

The boy never quite managed to look him in the eye. He chewed his lip and sidled around the corner to lean against the post that anchored the gate. "Cassie wants to know if you'll come to the house for supper tonight. Says to tell you she's got red beans and fried taters spiced up with onions and chili powder."

The excuse came automatically to his lips. "I'm too tired to clean up for supper inside tonight. I'll open a can of something out here and turn in."

Newt nodded but showed no signs of leaving, his hands filling the pockets of his too-big jeans. "I got something to tell you, Mr. Paradise. I've been learning to ride. Cassie's been teaching me during the morning time while you're gone. I thought maybe I could go out with you, earn my keep some. It'd sure make me feel better, Mr. Paradise, and I might be some help to you—not right at first, of course, but soon, I figure...if you'll let me go with you, that is."

Learning to ride, was he? Leon remembered evenings spent teaching Cassie to ride. He pushed those thoughts away—and Newt with them. "Naw, you better stick around and help out your sister."

"But there ain't nothing to do for her, Mr. Paradise," Newt argued. "Since we painted the outside of the house and beat the rugs and reorganized the cold cellar, there's just not anything for a man to do. Besides that, it's real depressing, Mr. Paradise. Freddy don't even make fun no more. Barton, he just keeps his nose stuck in those magazines of yours. Got to get it right up against the page to see the words, and he don't even know half of them. Cassie's got the twins looking them up in the dictionary for him, and it's so boring they fight over who gets to do it!" He snorted. "That's a sight. Neither one of them ever opened a book on his own before this. They always just figured books were to hit each other with."

"They've got to read in school, don't they?" Leon muttered, intrigued despite himself.

Newt grimaced. "Well, they didn't go much last year. Kyler lost his shoes in the bog, so they had to share Kole's between them. Pa figured it would teach them a lesson, but I reckon they were just as happy to spend the day on the creek bank or up the mountain."

Leon shook his head. "I'm surprised Cassie let them get away with that."

Newt looked thoughtful for a moment. "I s'pose it'll take a right strong man to make those two mind. Jos could've done it, and I reckon Pa could if he wanted to. So could you, no doubt."

Was there a challenge in that? Leon flicked his gaze up and back down again. "I haven't got time to haze two boys."

"Maybe if you'd let me come to work with you," Newt suggested hopefully.

Leon opened his mouth to tell him to forget it, then closed it again. What could it hurt to take him out? Likely he wouldn't last more than one day, anyway. Learning to ride around the corral was a shade different than spending hours in the saddle, moving over rough country and flushing out stupid cattle with unclipped horns. Besides, a stretch of fence way up north past the Lariat Arroyo needed restringing, and it was definitely a two-man job. Leon leaned forward, elbows on knees, and nodded. Newt whooped with delight.

"Now hold on there," Leon growled. "You haven't heard my terms yet."

Newt managed to contain himself. "Anything you say, Mr. Paradise, any way you want it."

As if he meant to have it any other way, Leon thought. He fixed Newt with a cool look. "You saddle your own horse and be ready to ride before daybreak. You bring along your own lunch or you don't eat, your own water or you don't drink."

"Yes, sir!"

"That's not all," Leon went on flatly. "You'll need work gloves, and wear something thick over your ankles so they don't rub raw. A single pair of socks won't do for the day we've got coming. And you'll do everything I tell you to do without a bunch of fool questions. You got that?"

"Yes, sir, Mr. Paradise, everything you say!"

"All right, then. You're going to need a long-sleeved shirt with a collar you can turn up and a hat."

"Got it."

Leon leaned back. "If you're not ready to ride when I am, you can spend your day in the house."

"I'll be ready, Mr. Paradise. You can count on me."

"We'll see," Leon grumbled. "Now get on out of here so I can get me some sleep."

The boy obediently left him. Forgetting dinner, Leon unbuckled his chaps and belt, pulled off his boots and shirt and turned in, bed being a blanket and a pile of hay. He slept poorly, but then it had been so long now—what was it, ten, eleven nights?—since he'd slept well that he didn't really expect anything else.

Nevertheless, crawling out of the sack that next morning seemed particularly difficult. He climbed up out of the hay, coughed to clear his throat and stomped his stockinged feet into his boots. It was pitch-black inside the barn, but he knew exactly where he'd left what, so he had no problem finding his belt, clean shirt and hat. Between stretches and yawns, he donned them, shirt first, then belt and hat. He slept in his jeans, undershirt and socks as protection against the cool nights.

He missed Cassie's breakfasts, but he tried not to think about it as he made his way to the two-burner camp stove in a far corner cleared of all immediately flammable materials. He turned on a fluorescent lantern and put some coffee on to boil, then hiked out into the desert a ways to relieve himself. He supposed it was foolish of him to keep living like this when he knew he could make use of the house at any time, but while this was more difficult in most ways, it was a hell of a lot easier on his pride. He wanted to stay out of Cassie's way. He couldn't stand the looks of pity and regret that she gave him, and the curiosity in the eyes of those boys made him distinctly uncomfortable. So why was he letting Newt tag along today? Ignoring the question, he swung by the windmill to quickly wash up and fill his canteens.

As he drew near the barn once more, he became aware of a small disturbance in the area of the eastern corral. Newt, no doubt, was trying to get a halter on a mount. Leon briefly considered offering a helping hand but decided against it. He wasn't going to fall into the trap of playing daddy to even one of Cassie's boys. He'd cut out his own horse the evening before and herded him into a stall in the barn. Saved time and effort on a sleepy morning. He went into the barn, blew the dust out of a mug and poured himself some intensely fortifying coffee, which he sipped while he packed away small cans of tuna and pork and beans, along with crackers and an apple. It wasn't the most appetizing meal he could imagine, but it was portable and on hand. Tomorrow he'd have to pay another visit to the cold cellar at a time when he could be sure Cassie wouldn't hear him and come down by way of the inside door to apologize one more time. He didn't think he could bear another of her apologies. There were only so many ways for a woman to say that she was sorry for not loving a man who desperately wanted her to.

He grilled some cheese toast, using stale bread and watery margarine, then wolfed it down and poured himself another cup of coffee to sip while he saddled up. Mechanically, he strapped his gear on the sturdy Appaloosa he'd chosen for that day. Called Mostly Ap, he was a single medium tan in front, except for a mottled splotch of pink on his muzzle. Then, midbelly, the tan became a cream color spotted with gray-brown. He was the ugliest thing Leon had ever seen, with a head that looked too big for his body and ears that would have done a jackrabbit proud, but he was smart and even-tempered and strong as a bull, without an ounce of quit in him. Leon left his cup on the corner post, combed his hair with his hands, settled his hat and led the horse out into the morning. It was still dark as pitch out with just the barest hint of lightening in the east, just enough to make out the line of the horizon. Leon made a surreptitious survey of the immediate area while adjusting his cinch. No Newt. He recognized an unaccountable sense of disappointment, then shook his head at himself. Was he so lonely these days that he'd welcome the inept assistance and largely irritating company of a hillbilly teenager?

Pushing aside such thoughts, he fitted his left boot into the stirrup and swung up into the saddle, adjusting his grip on the reins. Mostly Ap snorted and shifted weight, ears lying back, then popping up. Someone or something was around. Leon patted the supple tan neck and spoke comfortingly in a low, soft tone. "Guess we're going to have company, after all."

Clucking his tongue, he moved the ungainly-looking horse toward the corner of the corral. Newt was waiting there astride the sorrel mare Cassie sometimes rode. Behind him lurked the shadows of two more horses and riders. One of the mounts Leon identified by its ghostly patches of white coat as the skewbald gelding he'd brought in several nights earlier. His first thought was that Cassie had decided to come along, too, and he felt an immediate thrill at the prospect, but the next instant one of the twins, Kole, he thought, nudged his little Spanish Barb forward to the complaint of his brother, and Leon knew who was hoping to ride out with him that morning. He cursed in fluent Spanish, finally lapsing into English dotted with Spanish.

"What the *cuernos* do you two *asnos* think you're doing?"

All three erupted with explanations.

"We can go if Newt can!"

"They've been learning to ride, too, Mr. Paradise, honest!"

"We can do anything, if we set our minds to it, you'll see."

"He's not so much older'n us."

"Cassie'd have her hands full with these two if we left 'em, Mr. Paradise, and she's strung tight as fence wire now."

The last was all Leon really heard, and he knew immediately that it was so. Newt himself had told him that the boys required a strong hand, and he'd heard Cassie shouting at them several times, once, he recalled, for pelting Barton with horse turds. Barton, of course, couldn't see it coming. Leon turned off the idea that he ought to be taking Barton into El Paso to have his glasses replaced and stared daggers through the dark at the trio facing him. What was he going to do with them? Taking on one was bad enough; taking on all three was insanity. But what the hell? Maybe they'd entertain one another and keep out of his hair. And maybe snakes had tea parties. He was disgusted with himself because he knew he was going to ride out with all three of these outlaws.

"I'm going to have a lot of stars in my crown," he said disgustedly, "or else God Himself's laughing at me for a fool right now, and I wouldn't make book on which one."

The boys looked at him like he'd lost his mind, and he wasn't so sure they were wrong. Sighing, he pushed his hat back and leaned slightly forward, forearm laid across the saddle horn.

"All right now, you listen here. I'm not saying this but once. You'll do everything you're told the first time and you'll do it without griping. Otherwise, you can find your own way home again. Understand?"

"Yes, sir!"

"All right!"

"Yahoo!"

All three horses flinched, whinnied and danced nervously.

"Cut it out! Shut up! Of all the—" He bit off the angry words and easily brought his horse under control. The other three had a bit more trouble, but not much. Fortunately, the skewbald and sorrel were placid animals, and the Spanish Barb was well trained. Leon wheeled the big Appaloosa and moved him forward. "Follow me and try not to spook the horses into killing one of you!" he ordered. He could hear them grumbling at one another as they fell in behind him. Shaking his head, he set an even pace and rode without looking back.

They went east, the sky lightening gradually until the sun was well up, then turned north toward the arroyo. The boys were smarting off at one another in false whispers. He ignored them and rode on. When they came to the edge of the arroyo, he drew up and waited for the others to draw alongside him. There was only one way across this thing, down one side and up the other, but the way was steep and the footing tricky. He turned in the saddle and fixed them each in turn with a steely look. Lord, what a motley crew.

Newt was wearing a shapeless old felt hat of his that he'd thought Cassie had thrown out, ditto the shirt and jeans, which were held up by pieces of two belts linked together. Around his ankles and over the tops of his shoes were wrapped strips of fabric that Leon recognized as coming from a dress of Cassie's, one of the few she owned. He knew an intense moment of chagrin and then, an easing of something painful inside him. All right, whatever else she might be, she wasn't selfish, far from it. He remembered with a pang how she had resisted his efforts to spend money on her, and he knew now that she had been putting aside these old things for her boys. She had done everything for her boys, even marry him. She wouldn't have blinked twice at sacrificing an old dress of hers so Newt and the twins could play cowboy.

He looked more closely at those two scamps and could scarcely believe his eyes. One was wearing knit pants with a T-shirt under a faded, torn flannel shirt, a baseball cap and one—*uno*—boot from a pair he, Leon, must have outgrown about eighth grade. His brother was wearing the mate, along with an enormous pair of corduroy pants, a turtleneck sweater and an old straw hat that looked as though it might have belonged to Tom Sawyer. Their un-booted feet were wrapped just as Newt's were. He could just imagine the argument over those boots. Whose solution had it been to give them each one? Cassie. Cassie making do, doing her best. For a moment, a long, shame-ful moment, he couldn't breathe. Finally, he had to look away from them.

"I'll go first," he said, hoping no one else noticed the thickness in his voice. "You'll follow one at a time, one right behind the other. You get off the trail, you're liable to maim your horse and break your neck, so do just as I do, and no jostling for position. This isn't a game."

He headed out without so much as a glance at any of them, taking it slow and easy. Down the near side, across the narrow bottom, and up the far side, all went well. He could hear the creak of leather as horses and riders shifted weight behind him. Then he was up over the far lip of the arroyo and moving north. Behind him, one horse after an-other climbed up onto solid footing. He breathed a sigh of relief, and a second later he heard a scream, followed by a thud. He wheeled the Appaloosa in time to see the Barb dancing around over the body of one of the boys before taking off at a dead run. The saddle, he noted, was lying on the ground beside the boy.

Sheer panic descended. Oh, God, if he had killed one of Cassie's boys... The thought was so horrendous that he couldn't even complete it. He hit the ground, only to draw up in supreme relief an instant later as the downed boy sat up, groaning. The words Leon said then were neither Spanish nor fit for his mother's ears, and they were spurred by two things, his relief at seeing that boy move and the loose, unbroken cinch of that saddle. Why in hell had he not checked to be sure this pack of podunks knew what they were doing? Angry at himself, he stalked over to the boy and thrust out a hand, only to have the kid flinch and roll to his feet, coming up in a wary crouch.

"What the—"

"You hit me, I'll hit you back, I swear!"

Hit? Leon gaped at the freckled face, the owner of which actually thought he was going to get clubbed for falling off his horse! It struck him suddenly that that was exactly what they were all expecting. He straightened and looked from one to the other of them, taking in the anxious, defensive faces and balled-up fists. The sure knowledge that some-one had beat these boys for such accidents as this and maybe even less churned his stomach. He swallowed questions and expressions of pity, instinctively reaching out to them in the only way he knew how.

He squared his shoulders and looked to the wary boy. "The last time I hit a boy," he said deliberately, "I *was* a boy. And when I hit a man, you can be damned sure I've had deep provocation." He turned away as the boy re-laxed, looking to Newt and the remaining mounted twin. "Get down off those horses," he said, "and let me check those girths like I should've to begin with."

They looked at each other and got down. He checked first one saddle then the other, buckling latigos higher and tightening girths as he explained the proper procedures. "Any questions?" he asked, lowering the final stirrup. All three shook their heads. "All right," he said, "mount up and go after his—what's your name?" he asked the twin who had fallen.

"Kyler."

He motioned at the other two. "Mount up and go after Kyler's horse. He won't have gone far. Just get in front of him and wave your arms at him. He'll turn back this way. Drive him right through here. I'll get a rope on him." They were already clambering into their saddles. "Don't do anything chancey," he went on. "If you don't find him soon, just come on back. Hear?"

"Yes, sir!" Newt called, heeling his horse and bouncing off in the direction the Barb had gone.

"And do *not* cross that arroyo again!" Leon shouted after them. They waved their arms in acknowledgment and rode on. He noticed that Newt was finding his seat but Kole was just sort of hanging on. Some pointed instruction was due, he decided, but they were all game enough to make decent horsemen—just like their sister. He pushed further thought of her away, knowing it was something he was going to have to come back to sooner or later, and turned to Kyler. "You okay?" he asked.

The boy nodded his head and mumbled, "Sorry."

"What for?" Leon asked. "You did everything you were told. Not checking that girth and cinch was my fault. I'm the expert here, I should have made sure you knew what you were doing. I'm just grateful you didn't break your neck."

The boy was clearly agog. Leon chuckled, then climbed into the saddle and reached for his rope. "You ever swung a loop?" he asked the boy.

"No, sir."

Sir. Leon swallowed a lump in his throat and breathed past the tightening in his chest. "Well, pay attention then, and I'll show you how it's done."

They spent the next several minutes discussing the subject. Then a whistle alerted them to the return of the other boys, driving a winded Spanish Barb before them. Leon ordered Kyler out of the way, stationed himself and, when the Barb trotted past, dropped an easy loop over his head. Mostly Ap did everything he was supposed to, lowering his head and backing up to maintain the tension in the rope, until Leon silently ordered him to halt and swung down. The Barb stood snorting and heaving. Leon spoke softly and patted the animal's sleek neck, calming him before spreading the blanket over his back. After a few minutes, he lifted the saddle into place, then stepped back, motioning for Kyler to take over. The eyes the boy turned on him were absolutely worshipful. Leon could not resist dropping a hand on the boy's shoulder. Kyler grinned and went to work. When he was through, Leon clapped him on the shoulder again and boosted him into the saddle.

There were grins all around when they rode north once more, and Leon's was the widest of all. He didn't think anymore about dropping off the lot of them in El Paso and leaving them to their own devices. He thought instead of how many pairs of jeans and boots and hats were needed, of what lessons were required and when to begin them. He thought, too, that Widow Hatch's extra eight thousand acres might have to wait, and he hoped Cassie could stretch a dollar as far as he thought she could.

They were four tired, dirty ranchers who dragged in that evening, but Leon didn't let up until the horses were properly cared for, then he tossed all three of his "pardners" into the big horse trough out front of the barn. They tried to drown him by throwing water over the side. He pushed his hat back on his head and let them have at it, laughing as he hadn't done in some time.

"I see I'd have done better to bring a bar of soap."

Leon turned, laughter dying, to find Cassie at his elbow, an array of soft-drink cans arranged on the bottom half of a broiler pan as though it were a tray.

He turned away from her. "Boys, your sister's brought you something to drink. Come on up out of there before you ruin those boots." He gave each a hand, hauling them up out of the trough. They slung and dripped water, grinning ear to ear. Cassie clucked her tongue.

"I've never seen the like," she scolded good-naturedly. "You boys take your sodas to the back door. Strip off and put your clothes in the washtub, then get in the bath. I've got water heating."

"Aw, Cassie," the twins moaned in unison. "We want to shower off under the windmill like Leon!"

She shook her head stubbornly. "You'll take a hot soak in the tub and be glad for it," she told them. "Mark my words, you'll be too sore to move, otherwise."

"Do as your sister says," Leon ordered quietly, and the boys glumly turned and shuffled toward the back of the house. Cassie proffered the remaining soft drink in her hand, but he shook his head, not wanting to chance touching her fingers when he took it from her. She dropped her hand.

"Well," she whispered, "thanks, anyway."

He cut a sideways look at her. "For what?"

"Taking the boys out with you. They've been dying to go."

He nodded curtly. "No problem. Their help was welcome."

She made a strangling sound deep in her throat, a ghost of a smile on her lips. "I can imagine how much help they were."

He fought against a smile. "I managed to get a fair amount of work out of them."

"Good," she said simply, borrowing one of his trademark expressions.

He was reminded of the banter they'd enjoyed—*before* he'd had reason to believe her insincere—and resented it. "If you'll go back into the house," he said abruptly, "I'd like to take a shower."

The smile died on her lips. He looked away, somehow cut to the quick by that. When she turned, he found he couldn't let her go. Pride insisted that it was not for himself, though.

"Was it your father who beat them?" he asked quickly.

She stopped and turned back. "How did you know about that?"

He shrugged and narrowed his eyes, trying not to see how lovely she looked there in the waning daylight. "Kyler took a tumble. When I attempted to help, he practically came up swinging, declared he'd 'hit me back.' I could see that he expected me to take my fists to him, and that kind of expectation comes from experience. It was your father, wasn't it?"

She nodded, eyes averted as if in shame. "I guess I thought all fathers used their fists," she said softly, "but I found out otherwise when I married Jos." She lifted her chin almost defiantly. "He put a stop to it. Told Pa he'd beat him senseless every time he marked up Ma or the boys, and he'd have done it, too." Her eyes took on a dreamy quality. "Ma was happier than I'd ever seen her then."

So apparently had she been, and Leon felt his first genuine stab of jealousy for Jos Hunter. "What happened?" he asked, hoping to turn the conversation to other matters.

She shrugged. "Jos died, and then Mama took ill. Old Chintz didn't like watching her waste away, so he started staying out all the time. After she died, too, he went courting. Pa never could bear to be without a woman. He'd already picked out another one before Ma died, or so it seemed, but she married someone else. Then he took up with Marlene, and brother, did she lead him a merry chase! They got married after he got her pregnant, and it was obvious from the beginning that he was so taken with her, he'd do anything to keep her, and Marlene didn't like having all these Esterbridges underfoot. So Marlene got more and more impatient, and Pa got rougher and rougher." She stood looking at the ground for a long while, but Leon could feel that she wasn't finished. Finally, she whispered, "I had to get them out, and I knew you were more like Jos than Pa."

He snorted. "How could you know that?"

"The letters," she said softly. "The way you wrote about these wide-open spaces made me know that you had a wide-open heart. I knew I'd found someone special."

"Knew you'd found a meal ticket, you mean," he grumbled, regretting it even as he said it but unable to take it back and wanting her to convince him otherwise.

She simply stepped back as if he'd slapped her and stared off into space. He was on the verge of apologizing when she flapped her arms like a startled bird and started talking. "Dinner's on," she said in what he knew she meant to be a normal voice. "If you won't come into the house to eat, at least let me send a plate out by Newt."

He nodded tersely, unaccountably irritated. "Might as well. It's my food, after all."

She bit her lip, tears gathering in her eyes. "Leon, I know you want us to go, and—"

"Just send it out when it's ready," he interrupted sharply.

She clamped her jaws together and nodded, starting briskly toward the house. He wanted to stop her and wanted her gone at the same time. His own pain tied him in knots of uncertainty, but in the end he couldn't let her go like that.

"Cassie," he called out. She stopped and waited. "Me and the boys will be going into town tomorrow."

She swung around, fear on her face. "You aren't—"

"We need some things," he went on roughly, allaying her fears in the only way his anger would allow. "They can't go riding out looking like refugees from a church bazaar. If they're going to work, they deserve the gear to do it with."

The fear in her eyes softened into gratitude, but that wasn't what he wanted from her. "Newt's going to help me fix up the tack room for a sleeping space," he went on. "I'll be needing a bed. I'm damned tired of sleeping in straw."

To his surprise, gratitude was swiftly replaced with...anger? At what? He was being more than generous, to his way of thinking.

"Fine!" she snapped, turning on her heel and stalking away. "Buy yourself a bed, then! And...and sleep in it, for all I care!"

As if that wasn't the point! He gaped at her, hands at his hips. Of all the ignorant, strange, idiotic... Who could figure a woman, anyway? Certainly not him or he wouldn't be in this mess. Unless... But no, he couldn't believe she really wanted him in her bed. Still, it hadn't been all pretense, and nothing would ever make him believe that it had, though that was passing strange. He was going to have to think about that—later, when it hurt less. If such a day ever came.

Chapter Eight

When the phone rang, Cassie immediately jumped to conclusions. The truck had broken down. There had been an accident. One of the boys, or rather, the twins had pulled some idiotic stunt and gotten themselves arrested. Worse yet, Leon was disgusted with the whole affair and wanted her packed to leave by the time he got back to the ranch. The possibilities were appalling—and absurd, or so she told herself as she reached tentatively for the hand set.

"Hello?" The greeting was timid even to her own ears, and followed by a long silence. Finally, someone cleared *her* throat.

"Ah, excuse me. I must have reached a wrong number. I was calling the Paradise Ranch."

The conclusion Cassie jumped to next was as absurd as her earlier ones, but it didn't seem so to her. This woman was *not* Leon's mother. The voice was that of a much younger woman, an *attractive* woman—or one who thought she was attractive, anyway—and an uncertain woman, a woman shocked to hear another woman's voice on the line. She had to be an old girlfriend of Leon's—or maybe not so old a girlfriend. The idea smarted. Cassie folded an arm across her middle and assumed a cryptic tone. "Right number," she said shortly, "but Leon isn't here just now. He made a run into town."

Another long silence came, during which Cassie wondered if she ought to say more. She could reveal that she was Leon's wife, but was she really? He didn't seem to think so anymore, and she wasn't very hopeful that he'd change his mind any time soon. In fact, she figured she was living on borrowed time now. She had no doubt that as soon as Leon could work himself up to it, she would find herself a divorced woman. It was only his innate compassion, his goodness, that had kept him from it thus far, and that being the case, she couldn't deliberately hurt his chances with someone else. So, when the woman carefully said, "May I ask who's speaking, please?" Cassie adroitly ignored her.

"Could I take a message for Mr. Paradise?"

She could feel the woman's frustration, but she could feel, too, that she wasn't up to pushing for the information she wanted. She was correct. The woman meekly said, "No, thank you," and hung up. Now, what should she tell Leon?

By the time the truck drew up to the house, she had decided on giving him the bare bones of the conversation, but it was a while before she got the opportunity. It looked as though he'd bought out the stores, and the boys were in such an ecstasy of acquisition that they had to unveil, shake out and explain every item in detail. Leon had not neglected the younger boys, either. There were shirts, jeans, even boots for them. He came into the house to see how everything fit. It was all too big, but when he suggested taking back at least the boots, the boys put up such a howl that he dropped the idea. Cassie, for her part, could hardly speak.

"You didn't have to do this," she finally managed to say. "You don't owe us anything."

"No," he said matter-of-factly, "I don't," and he backed out the door and started walking. Cassie followed.

"Leon—"

"I have a lot to do before I can turn in, Cass. Send Newt out to help me, will you? We're going to share quarters in the barn—for a while."

"That isn't necessary!" she exclaimed. "If you won't move back into the house, *I'll* stay in the barn."

He stopped long enough to glance back at her. "And saddle me with that bunch of wild critters? Not on your life!" He strode on. She raced after him, caught up and clamped a hand over his forearm. He spun around, yanking free of her, anger and something else firing his eyes.

"Someone called!" she blurted out, anything to derail what sparked his gaze.

He glared at her. "Who?"

"I—I don't know. She didn't say."

"She?" He rolled his eyes, throwing his arms heavenward. "Oh, great! It was probably my mother! Now that's all I need! They'll be here by morning, no doubt. One look, and the lot of them will know—"

"It wasn't your mother!" she interrupted. "A-At least, I don't think it was. She sounded young, too young, anyway, to be your mother."

He lifted an eyebrow skeptically. "You're sure?"

She licked her lips, turning the memory over in her mind. When she looked up again, his gaze was fixed elsewhere. She twisted her hands together. "I'm sure."

His eyes lit briefly on her face, and he nodded. He clamped his jaw and shifted his weight to one foot, hands going to his waist. "All right," he said finally, "it wasn't my mother. Did she . . . insist on knowing who you were?"

She thought quickly, then shook her head. "She asked, but she didn't insist."

Anger flashed again. "What'd you tell her?" he demanded.

She lifted her eyes to his and left them there, wondering if he could see that he was breaking her heart. Obviously, he wanted no one who didn't already know of their marriage to hear of it now, especially his family. Yes, definitely a man working himself up to a divorce. Well, she couldn't complain. Though she hadn't *really* married him under false pretenses—she did love him, after all—he had every reason to think so. Besides, as he'd said, he owed them, her, nothing. "Nothing," she echoed softly, then quickly recalled herself. "I—I acted like I didn't even hear her, and I asked if I could take a message. She said no."

He seemed to accept that, mulling it over briefly. "Sounds like my sister-in-law Jeannie. I'd better call her back before that knife-tongued brother of mine shows up on my doorstep." He executed a 180-degree turn and marched into the house.

Cassie followed nervously. What would he tell his sister-in-law about her?

He made a beeline for the phone in the kitchen and made the call. In only seconds he was smiling into the receiver and saying, "Jeannie? How's it going, girl?"

Cassie crept around the room trying to appear busy but keeping quiet in the process. Leon shot her a wry glance.

"Yeah, I got the message," he said into the phone before turning his back on Cassie. "Uh-huh. Oh, that was just this little gal I've been seeing. Her, uh, car broke down out here, and I had to go into town for parts to fix it."

Cassie bowed her head, shamed to her very core. Leon shifted his weight from foot to foot.

"No, nothing serious," he said, his voice dropping. "I, uh, thought in the beginning that it might be different but... You know how it is."

Nothing serious. Cassie put her hand over her heart, too hurt even to listen to the remainder of his end of the conversation. After a few minutes, he hung up and turned uneasily to face her.

"Well, that ought to keep the wolves at bay for a while," he said, his voice rough.

She nodded and managed a weak smile. He stood there a moment longer, then turned jerkily and walked out.

Tears sprang to Cassie's eyes. She had lost him, and there was no use denying it any longer. It was just a matter of time now, and had been from the beginning. She couldn't blame him, and she would be eternally grateful for the time they'd had, for all he'd given her, them. With that in mind, she rushed to the front door and called out once more. "Leon!"

He barely broke stride as he stepped off the porch. "Yeah?"

"Thank you, for what you did for the boys."

He bent his head and lifted a hand in acknowledgment as he walked on. Tears rolled down her cheeks. He didn't want her gratitude. He didn't want anything from her. He was so good that he wouldn't let the boys go without, but not even a good man would saddle himself with a herd of youngsters not his own without sufficient reason. Try as she might, she hadn't given him that reason. She had loved him from the start with all she had, but it just wasn't enough. And now no one else would ever be enough for her.

Leon heard the rustle of movement in the pitch-black darkness of the tack room that was now his bedroom in the barn, his and Newt's. Why he'd let the boy move in here with him, he couldn't say. He shouldn't care that a refusal might have hurt the boy's feelings. He shouldn't care that the little house, *his* house, was bursting at the seams with Esterbridges and Hunters—and a Paradise. His wife. No matter what he had said to Jeannie, or Cassie, for that matter, he couldn't stop thinking of Cassie as his wife. Never mind that things had changed, never mind that though he had once believed, deep down, that she loved him. He knew now that she didn't, and that knowledge cut like a knife, and yet he hadn't quite come to the place where he could let go. Not just yet. Not until he could be reasonably sure that she, they, would be all right on their own.

He lay still, hoping Newt would settle down and drift off. The stiff new sheets he'd bought for the half bed scraped together in the dark. He sighed, a mistake, for it prompted the boy to speak.

"It sure is black in here without a window, isn't it?"

He sounded a little afraid of the dark, and Leon smiled to himself. "There's a lantern if you need it."

"Heck, no," Newt said, his voice whispery. "I like it. It kind of makes the room feel limitless, you know, like the range."

He knew, but he said, "Even the range has its limits, Newt. Everything and everyone does."

"Sure, but out here it doesn't seem like it. Everything's so wide open, it makes you feel ... free and ... big."

"Is that so?"

He imagined the boy had nodded because Newt's next words were not a direct answer.

"Back in West Virginia," Newt said thoughtfully, "seemed like we were living one right on top of another. Even out-of-doors with all the trees and creeks and cutbacks and overhangs and such, it felt ... tight, kind of cluttered up. But out here, seems like even the dirt's clean. A fellow don't feel all beat down out here. It feels ... right somehow. Safe."

Safe. That was easy enough to figure. At least here no one was going to take his fists to Newt just for living. Leon knew that was what Cassie had been after all along. She just wanted them safe. God knew that if she'd wanted wealth or an easy life, she'd have looked elsewhere after her first day here. That was part of why he'd felt the attraction had to be him. What else did he have to offer her but a lot of empty space and hard work and isolation? And love. But she hadn't really wanted that, just a safe place for her boys.

It hurt him to know that she'd settle for so little, that she was willing to do anything, give anything, for a bit of safety, even her body, her freedom ... And what did he want? Her love, only her love, for all that passion and romance to be real. Obviously, he wanted just about the only thing she couldn't give, though God knew she'd tried. Suddenly, he wished he'd never found out. He wished it had happened as she'd meant it to, with him none the wiser.

He was shocked to feel the tears on his face, shocked and ashamed. He rolled onto his side, his back to Newt, even though the deep darkness made him invisible. Yet, something told him that Newt could sense his despair, and he wasn't wrong.

"Mr. Leon," Newt said softly, "I want to thank you. Nobody's ever been so good to us, not even Jos."

Jos. The love of Cassie's life. Leon choked down the jealousy and made himself say, "Go to sleep, Newt."

He heard movement again, and then, out of the darkness, "I wish you wouldn't be mad at Cassie, Mr. Leon. She didn't mean to hurt you. She was just trying to take care of us."

"I understand that, Newt."

"She knows she did wrong, Mr. Leon. She says she didn't tell you the truth about us and things got all mixed up somehow, but she feels real bad about it. Sometimes she even cries."

Guilt, he thought. *It's the guilt that makes her cry.* He had been angry enough at first to want to hurt her, but not now. He had just been so hurt himself then that he had lashed out, and though he still felt this intense pain, he knew it was pointless to want the same for her. Cassie was never going to hurt like this because Cassie did not love him. That was what he really wanted, for Cassie to love him—as he loved her. He did love her. It came as something of a surprise. He'd been thinking all this time how she *didn't* love him, and now he knew that it didn't matter really what she'd done or how she might have used him, he loved her and that was why it hurt so much. He loved her, and no man wanted to hurt the woman he loved. He swallowed something thick and doughy that had gathered in his throat, and spoke.

"I'll talk to her, Newt."

He could feel the boy's relief.

"That's fine, Mr. Leon. I'm real glad, but...."

Leon smiled grimly into the dark. "But what?"

He took his time answering, apparently working himself up to it. "The thing is," he said finally, "she'd feel a lot better if you'd...move back into the house."

Leon lay there staring at nothing but blackness. The emptiness he felt, the yawning, painful emptiness threatened to swallow him whole. "It's not that easy, Newt." His voice was rough and gravelly.

"But if you're not still mad at her—"

"That's not the point, son. I can't explain it to you except to say that a man's got nothing unless he's got his pride. Even a man willing to be used has his pride." Even a man in love.

Newt lay so quiet for so long that Leon began to think he'd gone to sleep. Then, out of the still blackness he heard, "You've got so much to be proud of already, Mr. Leon. You've got the Paradise, and your good name for it. A-And you've built it up all by yourself. You're your own boss, Mr. Leon, and you spend your own money for other folk. You can ride and rope and build stuff and fix things and—"

"Newt," Leon interrupted, a great, heavy fondness for the boy filling him, "I'll speak to Cassie tomorrow, but that's all I can promise. Now hush up and let me sleep."

He heard the boy's smile. "Good night, Leon," he said softly.

Leon, not *Mr.* He steeled himself against the oddest yearning and thought of Bo, his younger brother. Soon Bo would be returning to Sul Ross, the state university in Alpine, which was exactly where Newt ought to be headed, too, but he wouldn't think of that now. He didn't want to think how uncertain Newt's future was or how bleak his own. He closed his eyes, and willed his soul to rest, blanketed in gloom.

Cassie slid the lid onto the heavy stew pot and turned off the butane burner beneath it. The cornbread was cooling on the table. She'd baked an apple pie after boiling the dried slices to plumpness. She stepped back from the stove, wiped her sweaty palms on her jeaned thighs and carefully adjusted the collar of her western blouse. The cutout in the center of her upper chest seemed daringly low and blatant, but she didn't care. Maybe he had gotten over his initial desire for her, but he had wanted her once. Maybe she could make him want her again. She had to try. Anyway, he had bought this blouse for her, picked it out himself, and she meant to give him his money's worth. Besides, they were married. For now, anyway. That could change, though, and soon, if he wanted to talk about what she figured he wanted to talk about this evening.

She took a deep breath and lightly smoothed her hair before walking across the kitchen and through the living room to the front door. Kyler and Kole were lounging on the sofa, playing gin with an old deck of cards. She turned to them, her voice stern.

"You two put those cards away. It's almost suppertime. I'm sending the little ones in, and you're to see to it they get cleaned up, hair combed and the whole bit. That means you, too. All right?"

They whined about it, but they folded up the cards. She shook a finger at them. "Don't touch that food until I'm ready to serve it up, hear?"

Kole scrunched up his face. "What difference does it make, he ain't coming in, no how."

Cassie set her jaw. "We'll just see if he won't," she said. "And you do like I tell you, or you won't be allowed to ride those horses for a week."

His mouth dropped open at the threat. Cassie nodded with satisfaction and went out the door. Pete, Freddy and

Barton were playing under the windmill. She shouted for them to get in the house and clean up, then turned grimly toward the barn. Her boots no longer felt heavy and cumbersome, but her steps dragged, nonetheless, as she crossed the wide, dusty yard. The barn was five, six times bigger than the house but no longer better organized. He could thank her for that much, at least. She pushed open the heavy rolling door a bit and slipped inside. They were in the far corner, currying the two horses they'd worked that day. The twins hadn't been needed, or so she'd been told. She had a sneaking suspicion that they were being punished for something or other, but she'd decided to keep her nose out of it. Leon could be trusted to be fair, after all.

She could hear Newt chattering as she approached, but as she drew near, he hushed. Leon sent him a look, and he tossed a blanket over the horse's back before hurrying off. Silently, Leon stroked the big black he was working on. Cassie draped her upper body over the stall gate and drank in the sight of him.

"Supper's ready," she said casually, and his hands stilled, an oblong brush strapped to each. "Stew, cornbread and apple pie. We were hoping you'd join us."

He slapped the two brushes together and dropped them into a bin with a hinged wooden lid. "Supper is not what I wanted to talk to you about," he said flatly.

Cassie tamped down her trepidation. "I know, but you have to eat, don't you? What could it hurt to take supper with us?"

He ignored her. Pulling a blanket from a hook on the wall, he shook it out and spread it over the horse. Next, he removed the bridle, then poured some feed and turned toward the rear of the stall. Cassie felt the impact of his gaze as surely as if he'd touched her, and it went straight to her chest. Despite her intentions, she straightened primly and looked away, the sultry expression she'd envisioned decaying into embarrassment. So much for seduction. She backed away from the gate as Leon walked toward, then through it. He let it swing shut, dropped the latch and leaned against it.

"I promised Newt I'd talk to you," he said.

Startled, she fixed her gaze on him. "Newt?" she echoed weakly. "This is about Newt?"

He bowed his head. "This is about all of us."

"Oh." She examined her fingernail, steeling herself.

After a long moment, he sighed, lifted his hat from his head and pushed his hand through his hair. "I know you were only trying to take care of these boys when you... What I mean is, I understand why you did it. I know it was for them."

She shook her head. "No, not really. Well, yes, in a way it was, but not like you think. That is, I meant to bring them out. I hoped you'd help us, but I didn't...*marry* you for them."

He lifted an eyebrow skeptically. "Didn't you?"

She took a step forward, desperately wanting to make him understand. "All right," she said softly. "It was partly for them, but it was *wholly* for me. I wanted to be your wife, Leon. I still do."

He looked down, scraping one toe against the dirt in the aisle between the stalls. "Well, that's what you are," he said, "legally, anyway."

That was like a physical blow. She caught her breath. "I want to go on being your wife," she said quietly, "in every way."

He looked up sharply. "You'd do just about anything for those boys, wouldn't you?"

She blanched. "Not that! I want that for *me!*"

"And what do you want for me, Cassie?" he asked, his voice rough and low.

"Everything good, Leon," she said entreatingly. "I want everything good for you. You deserve it."

"Gratitude!" he snapped, suddenly angry. "Well, that's not what I want for me, Cassie. That's not what I want at all."

"Then just tell me what you want, Leon," she implored. "Anything, just tell me."

His eyes were hard and flashing. "There are some things that just can't be had for the asking, Cassie. You just can't go back and do it all over again! You can't take away things that have already happened." He turned away, mumbling, "You can't manufacture feelings that aren't there."

She stiffened. Well, that was that, then. He didn't want her anymore, and there was nothing either of them could do about it. She swallowed convulsively. "You'll be wanting us to leave, then." The words came out in a near whisper. She felt the tears gathering in the backs of her eyes and wanted to be away from him before they started to fall. She strode past him, careful that their bodies didn't touch.

"Cassie," he said, but she didn't slow.

"I have to get dinner on," she managed to say over her shoulder. She hurried out the door and across the yard, blinking furiously. She couldn't afford to cry now, she told herself. She had to think, plan. She had to find someplace to go, but the tears were not obedient, and she was dashing them away with her fingertips by the time she got to the house. She stopped at the edge of the porch and sniffed and dabbed until the tears were held once more at bay. She didn't know that he was watching her from the relative darkness of the barn or that he was mumbling in Spanish under his breath.

She put on a smile and went into the house. Newt was sitting in the armchair, his wet hair slicked back, a clean shirt buttoned on over his jeans. He was calmly parting Petey's hair, also freshly washed, while Freddy stood at his elbow, waiting his turn. He looked up when she came through the door, and she saw the anxiety in his eyes. She brightened her smile, said nothing and walked through to the kitchen.

Kole had stacked plates next to the stew pot on the stove, eight of them. Someone, apparently, had convinced him that Leon would be joining them, after all. Newt, no doubt.

She bit her lip, thinking how disappointed he would be when Leon didn't show, but what could she do? Briskly, she took up the ladle and a hot pad, lifted the lid off the pot and began filling plates, which she transferred to the table, where Kole was busily laying out flatware and paper napkins. She could hear Kyler and Bart in the bathroom, giggling and splashing water in the sink.

"Food's on!" she called out. Several sets of footsteps could be heard coming from several directions. She filled the seventh plate, slid it onto the table behind her and lifted the lid back into place.

"Uh, Cassie."

She turned at the sound of Newt's voice. Leon was standing in the doorway, his hat in his hand, Newt to one side and slightly behind him. Her heart stopped. For a long, awkward moment, silence reigned, then Leon shifted his weight and nodded.

"Smells good," he said.

She just stared at him, uncertain what he expected. Newt cleared his throat and pushed past Leon to the table. There were only six chairs, but Cassie had laid a plank across two of them, creating an extra space. He lifted Freddy into that space, directed the twins to sit on either side of him and pointed Barton to a chair across the table before picking up the extra plate from the stove and shoving it gently at her.

Leon was actually going to eat with them! She turned quickly and ladled stew into the plate, then carried it to the end of the table and sat it down, indicating with her hand that he was to take that chair. He hung his hat on a peg on the wall and pulled out the chair. Newt took the chair next to Barton, leaving Petey and Cassie to share the remaining one. Cassie slid into it and patted her knee, reaching for the extra plate. "Come sit with me, son." But to her chagrin, young Pete turned expectantly to Leon. She watched them stare at each other, Petey looking up, Leon looking down. Then Leon stepped around the chair and dropped onto it.

Petey stepped up close to Leon's side and laid a hand on his leg. Leon just looked at it, the shock on his face carefully controlled, before glancing up at Cassie.

"Son," she said again. "Come on—"

But Petey was already climbing onto Leon's lap. She looked at Leon in dismay. He held his arms out as if afraid to touch the boy and equally afraid not to, while Petey crawled and rocked around until he found a comfortable position astraddle Leon's knee. He sat there a moment, then he leaned back against Leon's chest and put his index finger in his mouth. Leon looked at Cassie and then at the boys around the table. Finally, he picked up Petey with both hands and settled him on the other knee, wrapped an arm loosely around the small waist and leaned forward slightly. "Pass the cornbread, please," he said tonelessly, "and, uh, we'll need another spoon."

Cassie's heart was beating like a big brass drum, and she became aware—belatedly—that she was staring, her mouth ajar, when Newt hissed and inclined his head sharply, indicating the extra place setting near to hand. With a small cry, she snatched the knife and spoon in one grab and passed them down the table. Barton was the last to receive them. He peered at Leon uncertainly, then reached carefully toward the end of the table and attempted to lay the eating utensils next to Leon's plate. He laid them squarely in the middle, instead, his fist in Leon's stew. Barton's face colored as he slowly opened his hand and lifted it from Leon's dinner. Now Leon's mouth was hanging open. He glared at Barton incredulously, then he sent a stern look at Cassie.

"Take the boy into El Paso and get him some glasses," he ordered.

Glasses! Cassie's heart leaped. He was telling her that she could take... Oh. The flare of joy died. She got a grip on her fork and swallowed. "I—I can't."

His head came up again. "Can't?"

She licked her lips and watched him catch his breath before blurting out, "I can't drive!"

He stared at her as if he hadn't actually heard her, and then he abruptly sat back in his chair. The next instant, he lurched forward again. "Hell's bells, woman! You can't go on living out here without knowing how to drive!"

Cassie gulped. But then his words echoed through her head, and her own were out before she could stop them. "Am I going to go on living out here, Leon?"

He put his head down and glowered at her. The entire room seemed to hold its breath. Even Petey twisted around to stare up at him expectantly. Leon shot a look at Newt, then picked up his fork and stabbed at a chunk of beef on his plate. "Where else would you live?" he mumbled, popping the beef into his mouth.

Cassie literally sagged with relief, but she immediately forced her spine to stiffen, aware of the interested stares of six pairs of young eyes. It should have been enough to know that he wasn't set on throwing her off the place, but she couldn't help thinking about Barton's desperate need for glasses. She laid her hands calmly in her lap and fixed Leon with an impassive look. "Wh-what about Barton's glasses?"

An expression of irritation flitted across his face, but it vanished so quickly that she was left wondering if it had been there at all. He hunched a shoulder, concentrating on his plate. "It's obvious he can't see beyond the end of his nose," Leon muttered. "We'll take him into town first chance we get, but first you're going to learn to drive! It's insanity to try to stay on unless you do. What if one of these boys was hurt and I was out on the range? You could call an ambulance, all right, but do you have any idea how long it might take to get here? Survival could very well depend on your meeting it along the way."

Glances were traded all around the table. Eyes were wide. Finally, Leon picked up his fork again and began to eat. Others took up their utensils, and bits of food began to move from plates to stomachs. All but Newt and Petey, who seemed captivated by Leon's profile, ate in silence. It was Newt who fidgeted in his chair and cleared his throat, though. Leon looked up, pinned his gaze on Newt and laid his elbows on the table.

"Well?"

Newt pulled a deep breath. "What...what about me learning to drive?" he asked hopefully.

Cassie watched understanding dawn on Leon's face. "Oh, don't tell me...." His voice trailed off, then he slapped his fork down beside his plate. "What's with you people? Doesn't anybody drive in West Virginia?"

Newt's face flamed pink. Cassie gritted her teeth. He had no call embarrassing her brother! She swallowed a carrot and fixed her gaze on her plate. "People drive in West Virginia," she said tightly, "people *with cars.*"

Leon had the grace to look ashamed. He picked up his fork again. "We'll start tomorrow," he said. "I'll teach you both." He put down his fork again. "But somebody's going to have to do some work around here," he went on loudly, his eyes flickering toward the twins.

Kole gulped and sent a glance to his brother, who sent it right back to him before saying, "We...we could take care of the horses."

"A-And Petey and Freddy," Kole added, clearly wanting to impress. Cassie hid a smile. Whatever had gone on between the twins and Leon, they had obviously learned their lesson.

"And the house!" Kyler said. "We could straighten up the house!"

"Oh, brother!" Freddy exclaimed and smacked himself in the forehead. Unfortunately, the hand he used held his spoon, and his spoon contained a portion of rich brown stew gravy, which arranged itself in glops in his hair. Newt snickered. The twins laughed outright, while Barton leaned forward and tried to see what was so funny and Cassie tamed a wiggly smile. Petey pointed, his eyebrows arched comically. Freddy, while initially embarrassed, was quickly growing pleased with himself. Crossing his eyes, he stuck out his tongue and wagged his head from side to side, eliciting fresh laughter. Leon kept his head down over his plate, but Cassie felt certain he was hiding a smile under there. Finally, the laughter dwindled, and everyone but Petey went back to eating while Freddy sheepishly rubbed his hair with a napkin.

After a few moments, Leon laid down his fork and picked up the spoon, which he offered to Petey, who ignored it. Leon shifted his weight so that the boy looked up at him. "Take your finger out of your mouth," he said flatly, "and eat your dinner."

Petey stared at him as if mesmerized, then slowly pulled his finger from his mouth and reached for his spoon. Leon nodded and picked up his fork. Pete leaned forward on Leon's knee and began to eat off Leon's plate. When it was empty, Leon pushed it forward and lifted his gaze to Cassie. "That was good," he said. "We'd like another, please. And this time, pass the cornbread."

Cassie felt a stirring inside her, a warm, gentle, hopeful glow. She had to bite her tongue to keep from giving it voice, to keep from saying, "I love you," to the man at the end of the table. She took the plate and turned away, rising from her chair. As she ladled the thick, nourishing stew onto his—*their*—plate, she told herself sternly that his apparent acceptance of her son and compassion for Barton did not mean that he was willing to forgive and forget—yet. But it was a start, wasn't it? A beginning? "Please God," she whispered, "let it be a beginning." But when she turned back, her face was carefully blank. His was the same, but the gently nurtured flame of hope continued to burn.

Chapter Nine

"Relax," Leon said, sliding an arm around her shoulders. "Just relax."

Cassie gulped and nodded, painfully aware of his arm draped along the back of the seat and his thigh riding lightly against hers.

"You've got a death grip on the steering wheel," he said, his hand cupping her shoulder.

She made a concerted effort to loosen her hold, but his fingers slid against her arm. Her breasts tightened in reaction—and so did her hands.

"Loosen up some!" he commanded. "That steering wheel's not going anywhere without you."

Newt shifted around in the seat next to Leon and stared at her. Cassie felt color sting her cheeks. Why had she agreed to this? They'd been at this for days, and it was wearing on her. Newt, at least, should have stayed behind until it was his turn to drive again, then Leon wouldn't be plastered next to her doing funny things to her senses and distracting her. She took a deep breath, let it out and licked her lips.

Leon pushed a hand through his hair. "Will you please *relax!*"

Anger flared past the tears. "How can I relax with you yelling at me?"

The truck veered dangerously to the left. He made a grab for the wheel just as she corrected, and they ran off the road onto the sand on the right. Cassie screamed. Newt braced himself against the dash. Leon jerked the emergency brake, and they came to a jarring, wheel-locking halt.

"Out! Out! Out!" he shouted.

Both Cassie and Newt yanked door handles and released seat belts, tumbling out. Leon put his head down, linked his hands behind it and cussed in Spanish until he was calm again; then he slid beneath the wheel and out onto the sandy ground, eyeing them both balefully.

"All right," he said, hands going to his hips, legs slightly splayed. "Newt, you're going to stay here for a few minutes while Cassie and I drive down the road and back. Maybe without an audience, she—"

"No!" Cassie interjected, thinking how disturbing his presence at her side could be. "I—I don't want to learn to drive. I can't do it."

"You don't have a choice," he reminded her. "Living out here is dangerous enough as it is. Trying it without knowing how to drive is pure recklessness."

"I don't care!"

"Well, you should!"

He had a point, and she knew it, but her nerves were raw and hypersensitive. Her heart was still pounding, and she could feel the brush of his fingers lingering against her arm. She closed her eyes. "I can't do it."

"Can't do it?" he echoed, cocking his head to one side when she looked up. His voice and expression were cold. "You're the gal who went down into that ravine to free the steer, remember? You're the woman who got her young son and her five baby brothers out West to a new life, the one who got me to marry her in just under two weeks. I think you can drive a little old pickup truck.''

Her mouth was hanging open, but anger came swiftly behind the shock. ''You wanted to marry me as much as I wanted to marry you!'' she accused.

''Maybe so,'' he snapped, ''but you haven't given me a lot of reason to want to *stay* married to you!''

She stepped up toe to toe with him, aware of Newt standing to one side. ''I would if you'd let me,'' she said tersely, her voice soft.

He stared down at her, his expression slowly softening, but then his face hardened again, and he narrowed his eyes.

''You listen and you listen good,'' he snarled. ''If you want to stay on the Paradise, you get behind that wheel. Otherwise, I'm moving you into town.''

She glared at him, damning him with her eyes, and lifted her chin. ''Fine!'' she snapped, and brushed past him to the truck. She steeled herself, then determinedly climbed inside and jerked her seat belt across her body. He stayed where he was a moment longer, the rigidity of his stance proclaiming that he was trying to get a grip on his temper. Finally, he glanced at Newt.

''Wait here,'' he said brusquely. With a shake of his head, he wheeled and stalked around the back end of the truck to get in via the open passenger door. He slammed the door shut and slid over next to Cassie. ''Now,'' he began, ''first you—''

''Move over,'' she interrupted firmly.

He just stared at her. ''What?''

She turned her gaze out the windshield. ''I said, move over. I can't think with you sitting right on top of me.''

He gave her a long, curious look, then eased over to his right. ''Anything else, Your Highness?'' he asked sarcastically. ''Or should I say, Your *Hind*ness?''

She turned the full force of her glare on him. "If any-one around here resembles the hind end of a horse, it's you!" she declared. "Now shut up and teach me to drive."

"Kind of hard to do both," he muttered, properly chastened, but she ignored him.

"And buckle your seat belt. If I'm going to kill you, I want to do it with my hands around your throat!"

He straightened and looked down, ostensibly to fasten the belt, but she caught the ghost of a smile that he was trying to hide, and suddenly it was all right. She was going to learn to drive, and that was that. If he wanted to move her into town, he'd just have to find another excuse. In the meantime, she intended to give him as many reasons as she could to keep her with him, including being able to drive. Grimly, she put her foot on the brake pedal, released the emergency brake and set the transmission in the proper gear. She didn't even look at Leon before she eased the truck out onto the road.

Half an hour later, Newt was behind the wheel. Leon sat next to him, calmly giving instruction, while Cassie gazed broodingly out the passenger window. Newt, it seemed, was a natural, while she had barely executed the necessary maneuvers in an acceptable manner. Still, she had done more and better than she had first feared, and Leon had made no more threats about moving her into town.

Listening to his casual praise of Newt, she wondered bitterly if *all* her brothers would accompany her on such a move, but then she had to admit that Newt was not to blame for her problems with Leon. In fact, she had no one to blame but herself. Why, oh, why hadn't she handled things as she'd meant to? Why couldn't it have been a straightforward arrangement as she'd meant it to be? If only she hadn't fallen in love with him right at the beginning that way, they might have had time to work up to these finer feelings and there would have been no omissions, no misunderstandings, no disappointments. They might have been happy.

As it was, she could only see the barest, driest sort of future—unless she could convince him that her feelings were genuine, unless she could make him love her. But how to do it? She pondered that question during Newt's driving lesson, but the answers she derived were troublesome, some even a blow to her pride. Nevertheless, she gave each her fullest consideration. What use was pride if it cost her the most important person in her life? Just how Leon had become so important to her was no mystery. He was kind, decent, generous, hardworking and able, all things Jos had been, too, of course. But what drew her to Leon like a lodestone was the depth of emotion of which this man was capable. Maybe Jos had had that, too, and she simply hadn't been mature enough to recognize it. She knew that he had loved her, and yet, she had come to realize in those first weeks with Leon that Jos had always withheld some part of himself, as if doing so had somehow made him more of a man. Perhaps with time, he would have yielded that secret part of himself, too, but they would never know. Leon, on the other hand, had held back nothing—until she'd given him reason to question her own feelings for him. Now she had to give him reason to stay married to her—if this *mess* could be called marriage.

Lord, how she missed him! Even sitting next to him, her side brushing his, she missed the feeling that had bound them together as surely as any license or ceremony and certainly more firmly than the ring she wore on her left hand. That ceremony could be canceled, the license revoked with the signing of a few papers and the ring would slide right off her finger with the slightest tug. But how could she rid herself of this emotion? Maybe if he did to her what she had done to him ... She couldn't even imagine it. Leon was too good, too fair, too honest. Well, from now on she was going to be good, fair, honest, hardworking, kind, generous, loving... She was going to be everything he could possibly want, even if he ultimately wanted her gone.

* * *

Newt had done so well with the truck that Leon joked he ought to send him into El Paso with Cassie and Barton. However, since Newt didn't have a license—yet—the suggestion did not come to fruition. Cassie gave the boys careful instructions about what they should *not* do while she and Leon were gone. Then Leon gave them explicit instructions about what they *would* do. Even Petey was assigned chores. Leon told her later on the way to El Paso that it was easier to insure that boys wouldn't do what they shouldn't if they were busy doing what they should. It was irrefutable logic, and she told him so.

"Brilliant!" she said. "You're a natural parent." She received an irritated glower for her trouble. "All right," she muttered to the scenery flying by her window, "so you could learn."

They rode in silence for a while, but when they entered the interstate highway, Leon clicked the radio on and tuned it to a country station. Barton took that as his cue. Able to contain his curiosity only so long, he quizzed Cassie about what there was to see. When she ran out of answers, repeating the same ones time and again, he turned his attention to Leon. After sending her an amused glance over Barton's head, the man resorted to sheer fabrication. He saw all sorts of things beyond the boy's limited range of vision. Where Cassie had seen only wide-open space and great heaps of rocks, highline poles and barbed-wire fences, Leon saw amazing things, horses with unusual markings, coyotes unaware of the daylight, enormous snakes that disappeared down microscopic holes, cattle with record-length horns, even a horned lizard. "A horny toad," he called it, and he swore that it could shoot bullets of blood from its eyes.

He kept Barton entertained with that particular story for half an hour. Then somehow they got into a game of "gross out," with each one trying to outdo the other with stories of guts and gore, until Cassie called a halt to the play by threatening to throw up all over both of them. They unanimously pronounced that *she* was the champion "grosser-outer," and Leon started to sing along with the radio, supplying his own lyrics whenever any song seemed too solemn or serious. His lyrics got goofier and goofier, and Barton's laughter got louder and louder, until finally the boy was holding his sides and sniffing back tears. Then suddenly, they were in the city. It was the fastest three-hour drive in Cassie's experience.

Leon drove straight to a restaurant on the east side, and while Cassie and Barton ordered hamburgers and fries for the three of them, he went to the telephone and charmed the operator out of the address of the nearest one-hour optical service. A call to the shop produced the name of a doctor who could be trusted to work Barton into his afternoon schedule. Then a call to the doctor produced an appointment during the regular lunch hour. The trio gobbled down their burgers and spent a tense twenty minutes hunting for the doctor's office. The traffic frightened Cassie. Cars zipped through intersections at ridiculous speeds, and the city seemed to lack an adequate number of stoplights. She said a silent prayer of thanks that it was Leon behind the wheel and not her, but in the end, despite her distraction, Cassie was the one to spot the tiny shingle beside the door of the correct building, and they arrived only five minutes late.

Leon explained their circumstances to the doctor, who obligingly wrote not one but two prescriptions for lenses after a thorough examination. One prescription could be easily filled and would provide Barton the freedom to do most anything he wanted. The other would allow him to see in great detail even at a distance but the lenses would take longer to be correctly ground.

After the examination, the doctor turned them over to an assistant and excused himself to partake of a quick lunch. The young man in his proper white lab coat set about acquiring the information pertinent to his files. The first question proved a shocker, not the question itself but the answer that Barton quickly supplied. His name, he informed the assistant, was Bart Paradise. Leon and Cassie looked at each other in astonishment, but when she opened her mouth to correct the matter, Leon stopped her with a squeeze of his hand on her forearm and an almost imperceptible shake of his head. Her astonishment melted into silent gratitude that welled up in her eyes. After that, he seemed to avoid her gaze, but with Barton he behaved as if nothing extraordinary had transpired.

Cassie ached with love for both of them. Yet, she managed to keep her mouth shut and her hands to herself. No words of gratitude escaped her, no tender pats or smoothing of cowlicks, no desperate, clinging hugs. Still, she could not quite manage the nonchalance that Leon achieved. Too often, her smile was watery and her voice trembled ever so slightly. If Barton noticed anything out of the ordinary, however, he did not reveal it. Instead, he sat between Cassie and Leon with poorly concealed excitement as they drove to the optical outlet.

Choosing the frames proved to be something of an ordeal. Cassie was worried about cost, and Leon insisted on quality and Barton could only squint at his reflection in the mirror. Finally, the technician helpfully steered them to several pairs of frames that offered both durability and sensible pricing. The two that seemed to fit best were ordered, one to be fitted with lenses immediately, the other to be fitted with the specially ground lenses and mailed to Van Horn later, a pair and a spare, as Leon put it.

The promised hour was closer to two, but no one complained. Instead, Leon took Cassie and Barton to a grocery store, where they bought easily stored staple goods and half a dozen comic books, several magazines and a trio of paperback novels. Back at the optical outlet, Barton condescended to being parked in a chair and read to first by Cassie and then Leon, who did an admirable job of the required sound effects and, when the story palled, provided a demonstration of the action in the form of a short tussle and a pulled punch that quickly deteriorated into tickling. Cassie had never seen a man act like that with a kid. Chintz couldn't be bothered with mere children, and Petey had been so small when his father had died that Jos hadn't really had a chance to indulge in such games with him.

Cassie was amazed, enthralled and adoring. She wasn't alone. Barton was clearly attached to more about this man than his last name. Too old for actual hugs once the game was over, he settled for a casual, comradely draping of an arm around Leon's shoulders, even though he had to go up on his knees in the chair next to where Leon sat in order to accomplish it. Pretending ferocity, Leon wrapped an arm around Barton's neck, pulled him down and rubbed his knuckles against the top of the boy's head. Barton couldn't have responded with more joy, but what put the glow in Cassie's heart was the happiness on Leon's face. She hadn't been wrong. He *was* a natural parent, a truly gifted father, and she could see that he gave Barton something she herself could never have hoped to give him or the other boys, not even Petey. She saw, too, how right she had been to come to Texas and bring the boys here, even if she had gone about it all wrong, and she made a fresh vow to do her dead level best to keep this family together.

Family. Were they truly a family? She thought of Barton's giving his name to that technician at the eye doctor's office and mentally nodded. Oh, yes. Maybe they didn't all have the same last name, but somehow they had made of themselves a family of sorts, and God willing, one day they would have true little Paradises running around that twenty thousand acres that was home. If only her husband would once again start to think of her—and treat her—as his wife.

Bart was indefatigable. Cassie couldn't keep him indoors even at night. Now that he could see clearly again, he wanted to be out taking in the countryside and the sky and any and every thing they contained. When she complained to Leon and asked him to use his influence with the boy, he only laughed and said, "Think what it'll be like once those finer lenses arrive. Maybe we ought to buy him a telescope for Christmas. He could see for miles with that."

Christmas. He had as good as said they would still be here at Christmas! She had to bite her tongue to keep from asking if he meant it. But she made up her mind to do something she'd been considering since the trip to El Paso. It seemed the next logical step now that he was taking meals with the rest of them and even hanging around the house most evenings until bedtime. Yet, she was more nervous than she'd been on her wedding night, which was understandable, given the circumstances. Still, she wanted to approach him at the right time and in the right way. She decided to work up to it.

She took to walking out with him in the evenings as he left to bed down in the converted room in the barn. They made small talk, "family" talk. One night, Cassie told him how Barton had read the comics to Petey that day in just the same way that he, Leon, had read them to him, Barton.

"You're a good role model," she said, but he ignored that and talked instead of how much the older boys were learning about ranching, especially Newt. When she said that she was glad Newt could be of real help to him and learn useful skills in the process, Leon shook his head.

"That boy ought to be in college."

She was stunned at the depth of his conviction. "College?"

"He's an artist," Leon stated flatly. "If there's nothing else to hand, he'll scratch drawings in the dirt." He spread his hands. "It's a gift, Cassie. I knew it, I think, when you sent me that drawing he'd done of you, but these last weeks...." He shook his head. "I've seen Newt make the most amazing pictures on bare rock with the rowels of his spurs! He ought to have a chance to do what he's good at. He ought to have a chance at college."

She was flabbergasted. "I—I don't think he's even thought of it."

"Of course, he's thought of it, Cassie!" Leon responded angrily. "He won't say so, but I can see it in his eyes every time I mention it. He's like some starving kid with his nose pressed up against the bakery window!"

Suddenly, she was frightened. It was just so overwhelming. College! How could she think of finding a way for Newt to attend college when it had taken everything she'd had to put a roof over his head and food in his mouth? She certainly couldn't expect Leon to do it after everything else he'd done for them! She stubbornly shook her head. It was the end of enough. It was *too much*. "He can't go," she said. "H-He just can't go."

Leon turned on her, eyes blazing. "You tell him, then!" he challenged fiercely. "You brought him out here, so you tell him that he can't go! Otherwise, it'll be me saying it, even if it's never mentioned! Don't you see? You've made him *my* responsibility, Cassie. It's up to *me* to help him fulfill his dreams or crush them! And I didn't ask for it! I did not ask for it!" He paused to press his temples with thumb and middle finger of one hand, eyes closed. "I didn't ask for it," he said tiredly, "but I did let you make me responsible, and I guess I have to answer for that." He sighed as if bearing the weight of the world on his shoulders, and he was right. She knew that he was right.

She bit her lip. "I—I'm so sorry. I never realized—"

"You didn't want to realize!" he snapped.

She clapped a hand over her mouth to stop the trembling of her lips. After a moment, she removed it. "Leon, college was never a part... I never intended... I only wanted them—"

"Safe," he finished for her.

She stared at him, surprised, then nodded. "Yes, I wanted them safe. But I got so much more than that. They aren't just safe with you, they're *cared for*. My mother was the only person I ever knew who could care so much for other people—until you. I didn't know a man was capable of such caring, Leon, until you showed me. Oh, I got much more than mere safety for them, Leon, and don't think I don't know it!''

She clamped her jaw shut to keep from saying more, to hold back words that he probably wasn't yet ready to believe, to stop herself from telling him that she loved him more than her own life, to prevent her from begging him to feel for her just a part of what she could tell he felt for the boys. She stood there in the silence staring up at him, wondering if he could read in her eyes all that she felt, until he shook his head, mouth thinning cruelly.

"Damn you!" he said. "Damn you to hell," and then he turned and strode off into the night.

It wasn't any use. He was fighting a losing battle, and he knew it. He lay in the utter darkness, staring at the blackness, and tried to think of a way out of what he was feeling, trying to find out what he was going to do. But it wasn't any use. Cassie was right, and try as he might, he just couldn't find any way to stop caring, not for Newt, not for Kole or Kyler or Barton or Freddy or Petey. And not for her. He loved Cassie, and that was something he was going to have to learn to live with because he could no longer pretend, even to himself, that he had any intention of living without her. She had said that he wouldn't let her give him reasons to stay married to her, and maybe in a way she was right. Maybe it was his job to give her a chance. Maybe that was what marriage was all about.

He stopped trying to think of ways out, and started trying to think of ways in. He was tired of sleeping in this damned barn, tired of sleeping alone while his wife did the same. Actually, he thought she slept with Petey, while Barton and Freddy slept together in the little bed in the spare room and Kole and Kyler occupied the folded-down sofa in the living room. If he moved into the house now, someone was going to wind up sleeping on the floor again, and he couldn't have that. He thought about putting up another bed in the house, but there simply wasn't room. The house was, in fact, shockingly small for so large a family. They couldn't even all sit at the table together, unless he took Petey on his lap, which he found he didn't mind, but it could get awkward as the boy got older. He supposed they could always put another plank between chairs, but that wasn't what he wanted for his family.

Family. The word felt odd ratcheting around inside his head, but he couldn't say that he didn't like them. He thought of Barton telling that fellow at the optical outlet that his last name was Paradise, and he smiled to himself. Hell. He was lost the moment he'd decided to put them in the back of his truck and bring them home with him, and deep down he figured he'd known it even then. He no longer told himself that the only other thing he could have done was to leave them standing there on the street in Van Horn with no place to go and not a nickel between them. He'd had options. He could've called the state welfare office or a local church. He could've sent them to Dolores and Cutter as he'd offered to do with Cassie when she'd first come. He could even have driven them straight to El Paso, rented them an apartment and left enough cash to see them through while Cassie looked for work. And he could've seen a lawyer about a quick divorce on his way back to the ranch. But he'd done none of those things, and he wasn't going to do them, any of them.

He thought fleetingly of the Widow Hatch and those eight thousand acres with which she was willing to part, but he told himself he'd still be able to expand the Paradise—in time. Or he could take out a loan and do it now. Cutter would advance him the money, probably not without making some comment on how he'd managed to get himself saddled with half a dozen kids, but that was preferable to what Dale would say when he found out. And Dale would find out. The whole Paradise family would have to know sooner or later. Later, he decided, after he and Cassie had reached some kind of workable accord. He wanted to be able to present them with a stable marriage at the root of this unlikely family. He wanted to be able to present himself with the same, but he knew it meant swallowing his pride and settling for less than he'd expected from the relationship. *Well, so be it,* he told himself. *Better half a loaf than mere crumbs.* They could strike some kind of bargain. Now if he could just find the means and the words to do it.

By morning, he had a plan, but he decided the less said the better. Cassie would undoubtedly try to talk him out of spending any more of his ready cash, and he simply saw no other workable solution. He took breakfast with the rest of them, hotcakes with syrup, canned ham slices and crisp hash-brown potatoes well seasoned with onion and black pepper, then told Newt offhandedly that they'd be using the truck that day. Newt was disappointed. He loved working the horses. But Newt's disappointment was nothing compared to that of the twins. They knew they had no chance of being included in the day's doings when Leon left the house in the truck. They complained loudly enough to get Cassie after them and were up to their elbows in dishwater when Leon took his leave.

If Cassie noticed that he wasn't exactly dressed for a day on the range when he walked out of her house, she said nothing. As he drove away, however, the empty horse trailer hitched to the rear of the truck, he chanced to glance in his rearview mirror and saw that she stood on the porch, her hands wrapped in a dish towel, watching. He assumed that she would figure out soon enough that this was not to be just another day at work, but he told himself that it was for the best and put it out of mind as well as he was able. Newt was another matter, though. They were barely out of sight of the house when he turned an inquisitive gaze on Leon and came out with it.

"So what's up?"

Leon grinned. "What makes you think something's up?"

Newt made a face of disgust. "Come on, Leon, since when have we ever left the house towing an empty horse trailer—to town, no less—unless I'm mistaken?"

"No mistake," Leon admitted.

"Okay, so what's going on?"

Leon took a deep breath. "Two things," he said. "First, we're going to pay a visit to an old friend of mine, someone I went to school with. No harm in that, is there?"

"That depends," Newt said, eyeing him suspiciously, "on whether or not that friend happens to be female."

Leon nearly swallowed his tongue. He gaped at the boy. "No way! Where'd you get a fool notion like that?"

Newt had the grace to look shamefaced. "Well, you and Cassie don't exactly...live together."

Leon set his jaw. "No, we don't, exactly, but I've made up my mind that's going to change, which leads me to our second purpose today." He cut a look at the boy, who was all grins, and lifted his eyebrows. "We're going to the lumberyard, son. That house just isn't big enough for all of us."

Newt whooped as if he'd been given a new car. Leon chuckled and shook his head, but he almost felt like whooping himself. Almost.

She argued until she was blue in the face, saying over and over again that she had never meant for him to give away his chance at that extra eight thousand acres. He tried to tell her that he hadn't done any such thing, but she spied the receipt for the building materials in his shirt pocket and snatched it before he could stop her. Her face paled when she read the numbers written there, and it didn't help when he started talking about loans and such. Out of desperation, he simply took to ignoring her and went about his business, picking her up bodily and setting her aside when she got in the way. In the end, she sat down on the doorstep and wept. He shook his head and let her cry, more determined than ever.

Apparently, Newt was worried, though. He sidled up to Leon as they worked, his gaze on Cassie as she sat with her face hidden in the fold of her arms propped against her knees, and whispered his concern. "If she takes on like this over building on to the house, imagine what she'll do when she finds out about the other!"

Leon rolled his eyes. He'd argued this case once already that day and wasn't about to do so again. "It's just a college entrance exam, Newt!" he hissed. "Besides, you heard what Dutch said. Chances are you'll qualify for all sorts of grants and such. And he was the school principal, so he ought to know!"

"But college!" Newt whispered. "I'm not college stuff!"

"The hell you aren't," Leon muttered. "But you leave Cassie to me. Not a word until I have a chance to talk to her, understand?"

Newt nodded, but another problem immediately presented itself, rather, *two* problems.

"Leon?" Kole queried, glancing nervously in Cassie's direction. "Me and Kyler, we figure, if Cassie wants, instead of building on to the house, we can just sleep out here under the stars."

"We used to all the time, anyhow," Kyler added.

It took great discipline for Leon to keep his eyes where they ought to be instead of rolling them back in his head again, but he didn't want to hurt anyone's feelings, even if the offer was asinine. Besides, the twins had just given him the germ of an idea. He stopped digging footings for the foundation long enough to pat each boy on the shoulder. "Cassie'll come around," he said. "Building on is best. Trust me on this. All right?"

Both nodded glumly, and he told himself that he caught a flicker of relief in those identical eyes before he went back to work. He didn't work long, however. For what he had in mind, it was important that neither he nor Newt exhaust themselves on this particular afternoon, so he called a halt early, and sent the twins to the barn to saddle up two mounts. Then he whispered some instructions to Newt, and as soon as the boy went off to take care of them, he sat down next to Cassie, squeezing in the back door space with her.

He pulled out a handkerchief and offered it to her. She took it silently and mopped her face, sniffing, though the tears had stopped some time earlier.

"I never meant it to cost you like this, Leon. Honest to God, I didn't."

He nodded. "I can see that, Cassie, but I've given it lots of thought, and I'm convinced that this is best. Besides, it's done, so there's just no point in crying over it."

She sighed. "I can't help thinking that deep down you'll never forgive me," she said quietly.

He shook his head. "Cassie, it's not about forgiveness. It's about things not being like I thought they were."

"How do you mean?" she asked, narrowing her eyes as if trying to see inside him.

He almost told her. *It's about wanting you to love me like you loved Jos.* But it sounded petty even in the silence of his own mind. He shook his head and said, "Never mind that. The important thing is what we do now, Cassie, and I'm not talking about building on to the house. I mean you and me."

"You and me?" she repeated dully.

He looked down at his hands. They were shaking, so he looked up again. "I figure we ought to be able to work something out. We've got to make a real home for all these boys, after all."

"We?" she echoed weakly.

He looked at her, *really* looked at her for the first time in a long while. "Cassie," he asked gently, "would you spend the night with me, alone, out on the range, under the stars?"

Fresh tears welled up in her eyes, and her chin trembled, so that in the end she simply nodded. But then she smiled and laid her head on his shoulder, and when he closed his eyes and opened his hand, she laid her own in it.

Chapter Ten

He told her tales of the Old West with a strange, unhurried calm that seemed of no relation at all to the quivering giddiness that she felt. He spoke as they rode, his long arm sweeping back and forth as he pointed out where legend— or his own imagination—said that outlaws and posses and Indians had passed. He mentioned a few famous names and many others she had never heard before, telling tales of derring-do or simple survival or, most interesting of all, the details of day-to-day existence in a bygone time. Cassie listened with interest, but her mind was too full of the import of all that was transpiring between the two of them to allow her comment or question. She rode in silence, looking where he pointed or gazing at his animated face, stunned as his apparent contentment.

He had made a decision. It was as obvious as the handsome, aquiline nose on his face. He had decided to keep her and the brood she had brought him from West Virginia. Why else would he spend the money he had saved for buying land to build on to the house? Why else would he bring her out here, alone, for the night?

They rode up into the mountains and wound their way along a narrow, rocky trail to the top, where they made camp in a sandy spot flanked on the south by a pair of large, standing boulders. The view was incredible. They could watch the sun streak the sky with amber and pink and burning gold in the west, while in the east they could make out the shape and color of the big blue barn, catch a glimpse of the ranch house and windmill beyond, and watch the pale slash of the road disappear into the distance. The place was perhaps twenty yards across at the narrowest part, and it was sandiest just at the foot of the standing rocks. Leon dropped their bedrolls there and went about gathering small stones to make a fire ring.

Cassie was assigned the task of finding as much flammable material as possible. She came up with twigs and dried pods and even small leaves, quickly filling a grocery sack Leon had brought along just for that purpose. To her surprise, when she returned with the filled sack, he gave her another. "And this time," he told her wryly, "don't forget the dried cow pies you're likely to find."

Her mouth fell open. "You're joking!"

"Nope. They burn nice and slow if you bank them right." He chuckled at her wrinkled nose. "Don't worry. Your gloves will protect you, and one more sackload should see us through breakfast because. . . ." He shook out his bedroll, revealing several short pieces of scrap lumber. "I brought along some extra fuel."

"Oh, great," she grumbled perversely. "You gather nice clean blade-cut lumber while I go after cow pies!"

He shrugged and pushed up to his full height. "Okay, we'll trade. I'll gather fuel. You build the fire."

She rolled her eyes. "Yeah, right."

He laughed as she trudged off with the grocery bag. When she returned, he had a nice little blaze going and a skillet of oil heating over it. "You're through for the evening," he told her when she placed the first bag next to the other. "Supper's on me tonight."

It was a welcome respite, both from the responsibility of preparing dinner over a camp fire and from her unsettling physical awareness of him and the possibilities of the coming night. She walked over to a flat rock that jutted out over the side of the mountain and watched the last rays of light dissolve into deep blue, then purple, then gray, then black so strewn with diamond-bright stars that they were almost impossible to take in. It grew chilly, and she heard a strange rustling sound that seemed to come from beneath the very rock upon which she sat, then Leon called out that dinner was ready, and she got up to wander back to the campsite. Stepping down from the rock, her foot slipped into a hole in the soft sand at its edge, and she cried out. Leon was there in an instant, helping her regain her balance. She shivered.

"I heard something under there a minute ago."

He looked at the hole, which had been enlarged by her foot. "Probably a fox," he said. "We've got gray foxes around here. I used to try to keep a few chickens, but the foxes and coyotes kept getting them. Nothing to worry about."

She nodded and allowed him to lead her back to the camp fire. He'd cooked up quite a feast, hot vegetable soup from a can, grilled ham-and-cheese sandwiches, and fried cornbread patties. She sat down, feeling warm and cozy despite the chill in the air. They drank their soup from the cans and managed their sandwiches and cornbread with paper napkins, which could be burned when they were done. That kept the cleanup to a minimum. Leon scrubbed the cans and skillet with sand, then rinsed them with water before packing them away. That done, he moved the horses to fresh forage and secured them for the night, then returned to the fire to stretch out on his bedroll, his arms folded behind his head.

"Well," he said, "I guess we've avoided it as long as we can."

She didn't pretend to misunderstand him. "What was it you wanted to say, Leon?"

He thought a moment, then shrugged. "I guess I just want us to work something out about this marriage. It's no secret that I've been...uncertain. Guess my pride took quite a beating when I found out why you married me."

"I'm sorry, Leon. It wasn't how it looked, you know. I mean, I did want to make a home for the boys, but that wasn't the only reason I married you."

"No?"

"Honestly, I couldn't believe my luck. You're so much more than I ever hoped to find. I was thrilled, delighted to marry you."

"Because I'm such a nice guy, no doubt," he said cryptically.

"You are a nice guy," she told him sincerely.

"Yeah, but you'd have married me if I was a grumpy old goat with a glass eye, so long as I took those boys, wouldn't you?"

She didn't answer. She didn't have to.

He sighed and tossed a pebble at the fire. "Answer me one question, Cass. Was it all pretend, you and me?"

"No! You know it wasn't."

"Do I?"

"How can you doubt it?" she asked, leaning forward on her hands. "It was so good. At least it was for me."

He lay back and looked up at the night sky. When he spoke, it was slowly and calmly. "If that's the case, then you won't mind sleeping with me again."

"No," she whispered, moved almost to the point of tears. At last, he understood how much she cared. At last, they could be husband and wife again as they were in the beginning. "I won't mind. Far from it."

"Good," he said, "because I think you owe me that much, Cass."

She went cold. Owed? He felt she owed him sex? That's what this was about? He sat up, his arm draped over a drawn up knee. She knew her face looked stricken and quickly turned away.

"What's wrong?"

Wrong? Only that she loved him and wanted to be loved in return. But did she have any right to that? From the time she'd left West Virginia, she'd intended to exchange all wifely duties, including sex, for security for herself and the boys. Why then did it sound so repugnant now? How could it hurt like this? The irony of the situation struck her with the force of a sledgehammer. It had seemed a fair, reasonable trade when he had been just a means to an end, but she hadn't loved him then. Now that he owned her heart, nothing could have seemed more unfair or painful. But she had made her bed, and now it was time to lie in it. She made herself put on a smile and turn it to him.

He took her in his arms and pulled her close, his mouth finding hers unerringly. It was such a bittersweet thing, so longed for and so wrong. She told herself that she had no right to refuse him, that she could pretend all was as it had been. She still loved him, after all, and he might well come to feel love for her if she didn't disappoint him, if she was a good wife. She wanted to be a good wife. Yet, the tears still escaped her tightly closed lids and rolled down her face.

He thrust her away from him and sprang to his feet, hands going to his hips, head bent in disgust. "Oh, you don't mind, you just can't stand for me to touch you!"

"It's not that!" she cried, but he was striding away. "Leon, please!" He stopped as if he was about to turn back, but then he strode on and was swallowed up by the dark. She sat down on the sand with a plop, wrapped her arms around herself and wept for a long while, the tears rolling silently down her face to drip from her chin onto her lap. Cried-out and shivering as the fire died down, she crawled into her sleeping bag and finally drifted into a fitful sleep.

The sky was tinged with gold when she woke, but it was not the sun that pulled her from uneasy dreams. Rather it was the chill that hung in the predawn air. She snuggled deeper into her bag, then rolled onto her side, relieving cramped muscles. Leon lay with his back to her, buried in his sleeping bag up to his ears, a long, gray-gold stick lying next to him. Then the stick moved, rippled ever so slightly and bunched up. *Snake.* The word slammed through Cassie's consciousness.

Unthinkingly, she bolted up to her knees and would have gained her feet in that one movement if the sleeping bag hadn't hampered her. The snake coiled and began its rattle, softly at first, then louder. Paralyzed, she waited, open-mouthed, for its next move. The flat, ugly head waved from side to side, tongue slithering in and out of its mouth. The bag had fallen down around her waist, and she did not dare adjust it to afford her more protection. She wanted to hide her hands, which were uncovered, but remained as perfectly motionless as her fear would allow. After what seemed an eternity, the snake slowly lowered its head and moved, not toward her, but to Leon. Panic seized her, yet she remained frozen, her stomach roiling, her muscles leaden, as inch by inch the snake crawled up Leon's back. If he should awaken and move... She couldn't bear the thought, couldn't allow the possibility. She feverishly ticked off her options and found only one that would not put Leon in greater danger. When the snake reached the crest of Leon's shoulder, its head bowed up and away from Leon's body. Cassie closed off thought and acted. When her hand closed around the snake just below its head, she screamed, hating the feel of it and knowing that if she dropped it, she or Leon would be bitten.

Leon sprang up, eyes wild, and gaped at what he beheld. She had a death grip on that snake, and her stomach was lurching. She gulped down the bile and gasped for breath, trembling from head to toe but not daring to loosen her hold. Leon fought his way up out of the sleeping bag, cussing in English, having temporarily forgotten his Spanish. It was then that the snake began to thrash.

"Don't move!" As if she could. "God in heaven!" He raked his hands through his hair, shifting his weight from side to side. He licked his lips, frantically trying to think.

The snake curled up and over her arm. She screamed again and fell back upon her heels but somehow maintained her grip. Leon reached for her, then drew back. "All right. All right," he said, trying to calm her. "Listen. As long as you hold on, it can't bite you. Now...now...." He looked around them and seemed to come to a decision. "Here's what we're going to do," he said, moving slowly forward. "We're going to throw it over the edge of the mountain."

"H-How?" she panted.

He eased closer. "I'm going to help you up. Then we're going to walk together to that flat rock over there, and when we're close to the edge, I'll pull it off your arm and together we'll throw it over the side. All right? Understand?"

She nodded, concentrating on maintaining her hold, on not allowing that snake to work its head even a fraction of an inch higher. Leon inched around to the side and slowly laid his hands on her upper arms. The snake opened its jaws wide and hissed, fangs bared, but Cassie held on. Leon lifted her and kicked the sleeping bag aside as she got her feet beneath her. They practically ran to the flat rock, steps matched, Leon's hands never leaving her shoulders until they'd reached the edge. Cassie was sobbing, though her eyes were dry, as he peeled the snake from her arm.

"On three," he said, looking into her eyes while the snake rippled and hissed. "One, two, three!"

She thrust the hated thing away from her, opened her hand and yanked back. Leon's arms had already come around her, and they scrambled together down off that rock and away. They stumbled over the ashes of their fire before they came to a halt, and then he pulled her against him and held her tight.

"Are you all right?"

"It almost bit you!" she exclaimed, tears flowing now in her relief.

"Me? What about you?" First he shook her, then hugged her tight. "How in blue blazes did you get hold of that thing?"

She started to explain, stammering over the words as he examined her hands and lower arms.

"You should have let it bite me," he said, voice trembling. "It would've hurt less than the heart attack you gave me when I saw you holding the damned thing!"

"I couldn't," she whispered. "I just couldn't."

Then, he turned her face up and kissed her, gently. "God, if anything had happened to you...."

"That's just what I was thinking about you," she said, hugging him.

"We're both okay, thanks to you."

"And you."

He chuckled. "Okay, so we're a couple of heroes. Now, let's get out of here. I'm not feeling much like breakfast right now."

"Me, neither. I want to wash my hands."

"Gee, I can't imagine why, after wrestling a rattler barehanded."

She laughed at that, and he smiled, loosening his embrace and backing away. She sighed, blessedly calm. He quickly started breaking camp, and she began to help him, eager to be home. They hadn't settled anything, but somehow that didn't matter. She wasn't about to give up. She had fought a rattlesnake for him, and she'd be hanged if she'd let him go after that! One way or another, she was going to win his heart, no matter what.

Leon carefully moved and packed up the gear, on the lookout for any more snakes but not wanting to tell Cassie that it was possible they'd camped right next to a den of rattlers. That sound she'd heard beneath the rock the night before was bothering him. Had he been too quick to dismiss it as harmless? He'd never know for sure, but if he had, it could have cost him dearly. It could have cost him Cassie! He didn't even want to think about it. He just wanted to get her out of there safely and quickly. The whole thing had been a bust, anyway.

Some seduction! She'd cried when he'd kissed her. Cried! And he couldn't figure out why. She hadn't seemed to mind his kisses *before*. In fact, she had seemed to like them. A great deal. He was the one who had moved out of the house and the bed they'd shared. He just hadn't been able to bear the notion that she was sleeping with him as some kind of payment for taking in the boys. Payment. *You owe me that much.* Lord, had he actually said that?

He tried to think, to recapture the moment in his mind. *I think you owe me that much, Cass.* There had been an instant of what? Pain? Disappointment? And then she'd turned away, only to turn back a moment later with a smile that he now recognized as patently false. He packed up, made sure the fire was absolutely dead and took her with him to saddle up the horses, wanting her as far away from that flat rock as possible. All the while, he kept mulling over in his head not only what had happened the night before, but a great many other things, like the way she had loved him in the beginning, wildly, freely. He remembered how she had looked at him with her eyes lit up and smiling from deep down inside, how she'd slept curled around him and whispered that she loved him. Loved him. Was it possible, or just wishful thinking?

He bent his mind around that question as they mounted up and rode. She had undoubtedly meant to marry him and foist those boys on him from the beginning. She'd been desperate enough to do it even if she'd despised him. But she didn't despise him. She couldn't have reached out and latched on to that rattler if she despised him. In fact, he wouldn't have bet money that she would have been able to do it under any circumstances. The woman had pluck for sure, but enough to make herself do something like that? Maybe if she'd had time to work up to it, but not instantly like that. He didn't quite know what to think, except that she'd grabbed that snake rather than let it bite him and that she hadn't turned her head away or put on false smiles or cried when she'd thought, known, that he loved her. And she had to have known, didn't she? Come to think of it, he wasn't sure he'd ever told her. Maybe if he had, things would be different now. He hadn't reached any solid conclusions by the time Cassie lifted a hand and pointed toward the east. "I think we've got company."

The sun was full up by then, and they were halfway down the mountain. He didn't have any trouble spotting the plume of dust that moved along the road toward the ranch house or recognizing the vehicle that caused it. Dale. That was Dale, sure as shooting, and maybe his parents, as well. He closed his eyes and called to mind every Spanish word he knew. There wasn't a chance in a million that they could reach the house before Dale did, and he shuddered to think what kind of story his bossy brother was going to get out of the boys. Well, he had no one to blame but himself. He should have delivered the news in his own way long ago, but he'd put it off rather than deal with it. Fine way for a man to act, a man with a family of his own, at that. He looked to Cassie and shook his head apologetically.

"Two snakes in one morning," he said.

She just stared at him. "What are you talking about?"

He sighed. "That's my brother."

"Oh. Well, we'd better get back to the house to meet him, then, hadn't we?"

He nodded grimly and led the way, keeping the horses to a careful walk until they had gained level ground. "Up to a fast ride?" he asked.

She gave him a smile. "Hey, I'm the girl who rescues steers, and wrestles rattlers, remember?"

He shook his head, grinning, and touched his heels to his mount's flanks. They were off in a flash, Cassie right behind him. He set a healthy pace, fast but not too fast. He didn't want to kill his horses or, worse yet, Cassie, but he needn't have worried. The horses were up to the run, and Cassie was up to the ride, as he should have known she would be. He could only hope she was up to Dale, because it wasn't likely to be a pretty scene once his overly protective brother got the picture.

They pulled up and trotted into the yard. Leon was relieved to see his mother standing near the corner of the porch. Dale would at least make an effort to control himself with her there. Her head was bent as she listened to something Freddy was telling her. Freddy. Oh, Lord. Well, it couldn't have been too bad, she was laughing, her hand over her mouth. Just then, he caught sight of Dale striding around the side of the house, an animated Barton at his elbow, showing off the new addition, no doubt. His father was there, too, on the porch with the twins. Quite a gathering. Only Newt and Petey were missing, but not for long. They stepped out of the house, Newt carrying Petey, just as Leon swung down off his horse.

He instinctively stepped over to help Cassie dismount, not because she needed help but because he was feeling particularly protective at the moment, and yelled to the twins to come and take the horses. Thankfully, Kole and Kyler obeyed without complaint, as if they were actually used to doing so. Leon noticed that they shot him nervous looks as they led the horses away, but he didn't have time to consider what that might be about. He had an explosion to head off, if possible, and he wouldn't do it by behaving defensively. Best to act as if everything was fine.

"Hey, folks!" he called out, walking toward the house. "Good to see you. You should've let us know you were coming. We'd have been here to greet you."

"Actually," his father said, stepping to the edge of the porch, "Dale called last night."

Newt stepped up beside him, saying apologetically, "The twins took the call. I was bathing the runts."

"Ah." Well, that explained why his people had set out for his place before daylight. No doubt the twins had spilled their guts, answered Dale's every question with the absolute truth, unless they could've thought of something worse. He put a hand to the back of his neck, aware that Cassie had come to stand at his side. There was only one thing to do now. "Mom, Dad, I want you to meet someone." He slid an arm around her shoulders. "This is Cassie... my wife."

No one seemed surprised. Cassie nodded congenially, her hands twisted together. "Ma'am, sir, pleased to meet you."

May Paradise looked to her husband. "Well," he said, "she's a pretty one. Wouldn't have expected less under the circumstances."

Leon felt Cassie stiffen and shot her a worried look. "We should have called you," he said a little too loudly. "We just... There was just so much to do, with the boys and all." It was the wrong thing to say.

"We noticed you have a houseful," his mother commented softly, her eyes shining as if she might cry.

"My brothers," Cassie said quickly. "Except the little one. He's my son. Petey."

"Quite a ready-made family," Mr. Paradise said.

Dale stepped around the corner of the house and up onto the porch. "Yes, sir, quite a crew." He was much like Leon, a few pounds heavier, a bit more sunburned, with a touch of silver threaded into his hair at the temples. He pushed his hat back on his head and folded his arms, leaning casually against the porch post. "You've done some damned dumb things in your life, little brother," he said, "but this takes the cake!"

Leon felt his temper ignite and made a valiant effort to hold on to it. "Look, Dale," he said through clenched teeth, "we agreed to disagree when I bought this place—"

"You should've stayed home."

"*This* is my home. The Far Gone is yours, and that's only fitting, as you're the oldest. The Paradise is—"

"A bunch of sand and rock!" Dale said. "Nobody asked you to leave the Far Gone for this!"

"I know that! I wanted my own place, and I got it, and it's a damned fine place, no matter what you think!"

"I think you've lost your ever-loving mind, getting yourself saddled with a bunch of kids and a woman you met through an advertisement! What's wrong with you? Have you lost the little sense God gave you? Advertising for a wife! That's about as dumb as moving off out here in the middle of—"

"Don't you talk to him like that!"

Leon didn't know who was more surprised, him or Dale. He was set to smack the blowhard in the jaw and up steps Cassie, her arms stiff at her sides, hands balled into small fists—the same hands that had grabbed a snake to protect him earlier! He looked at her, and suddenly he knew she'd fight Satan himself for him. And there could only be one reason for it.

Dale could have fallen off the face of the earth at that moment, and Leon wouldn't have cared or noticed. He reached out for his wife's hand, but she shook him off and stepped forward, her whole being concentrated on Dale.

"Don't you ever talk to him like that again!" she repeated. "You're not fit to wipe his shoes, let alone cut up at him!"

"Cassie—"

"I won't have it, you hear? Why, he's the finest, the most generous, wonderful... And it wasn't his fault at all! He didn't know he wasn't getting just a wife! And it didn't matter about Petey, because that's the kind of man Leon is!"

"Honey...." He put a hand on her arm and turned her toward him, but she just screwed her neck around and glared at Dale, whose mouth was hanging open in shock.

"Would you make a home for these boys?" she demanded. "I think not! No, you'd be too busy telling me what a fiend I was for springing them on you! Never mind that they didn't have anywhere else to go or anyone to go to or—"

"Cassie!"

"Well, it's not right," she cried, "him saying those things to you when—"

"Cassie, I love you."

"—you've only tried to do the best thing for everybody, using the money you'd saved for the extra land, sleeping in—"

He shut her up the only way he knew how. There were *some* things better left unsaid, after all, and he wanted so badly to be kissing her, anyway. It took a moment for her to realize what was going on, but when she did, she closed her eyes and relaxed against him, her arms coming up to clasp him to her. He'd have gone on kissing her if his father hadn't cleared his throat and Petey hadn't started giggling. As it was, he couldn't quite let go, so he just lifted his head and glared at the lot of them. Newt was grinning like an idiot. The twins were there, and they were shoving each other and making snide remarks under their breath. Freddy rolled his eyes and smacked himself in the forehead. Barton had come up beside Dale and was looking at them as if they'd lost their minds, his eyebrows hitched up over the tops of his glasses. And his mother...his mother was smiling.

"Of all the things!" Dale groused.

His mother and Cassie said it at the same time, "Shut up, Dale!" and then they looked at each other in surprise.

Leon started to laugh, but got hold of himself quickly enough to say, "Uh, Newt, why don't you take everyone inside and...feed them...or something."

"I'll make breakfast," May said calmly, "then we can all have a nice visit and get that extra room up." She sent a meaningful look to her eldest son, who squirmed visibly beneath it.

"Well, sure," Dale mumbled, "never meant to say we wouldn't help out."

"What family's for," his father announced.

"Thanks," Leon said, dividing a grateful look between them. "If you don't mind, I'd like to have a word with my wife . . . in the barn. Make yourselves to home. We'll be in directly. Boys," he added, "best behavior."

"They'll do fine," May said, herding everybody into the house. "I'll see to it. Y'all take your time."

He could have kissed her, if it hadn't meant letting go of Cassie. Instead, he tried to tell his mother with a look how grateful—and pleased—he was. May smiled knowingly and shooed Dale toward the door.

"What is going on?" he hissed. "That woman—"

"Obviously loves him," May said sternly, "and that's all that counts."

Leon turned Cassie toward the barn, anxious to have her alone, to say everything he should have been saying all along, to touch her as he should have, could have been doing from the beginning. She looked back over her shoulder, biting her lip.

"Are you sure we shouldn't—"

"I'm sure," he said. "March."

She turned up soft, slightly troubled eyes at him, letting him steer her toward the barn. "I don't know what came over me," she said. "I just got so mad."

He grinned and pushed her head down onto his shoulder. Her arm was around his waist, and he held her tightly against his side as he walked her across the yard. "It doesn't matter. I just want to tell you something, again, only in private this time, so I can be sure you hear me."

"What's that?"

They had reached the barn, and he led her inside, rolled the door closed and turned her against it, planting his hands on either side of her head, just above her shoulders. "It's like this," he said. "I've been a damned fool. I love you, Cassie, and I know—"

"Leon!" She threw her arms around him so hard she nearly knocked him off his feet. "Oh, Leon, I love you, too! I always have! Right from the start! How could I not? You're the finest man I've ever known!"

He cupped her face in his hands. "The finest?" he said, feeling that his heart had swelled so that it was choking him. "Finer even than Jos?"

"Jos? I don't know. I guess we weren't together long enough so I could know, or maybe I was too young. I only know that, good as he was, he never made me feel like you do, like I'd die if you didn't come to love me!"

"Oh, Cassie, honey, that's exactly how I've been feeling about you."

"It was my fault," she said. "I meant to make a kind of bargain with you once I was sure we'd suit, to be your wife in return for your taking us in. But once I got here, you were just so much more than I could ever have hoped, and I started to love you. Then I was afraid to tell you about the boys for fear you'd send me away, so I decided to kind of work them in one at a time, even though I knew they couldn't stay much longer with Pa and Marlene. Problem was—"

"Your father turned them out before you could make a place for them," he finished saying for her.

"And there was nothing I could do to convince you how I felt, because the truth was that I meant to settle them on you from the beginning. I just never meant to fall in love with you. It happened so quick. I just...I don't know, I guess it was love at first sight or something, very nearly, anyway."

"Same for me," he said. "I kept telling myself to go slow and be real sure, but my old heart just wouldn't behave. It had to have you, even when I thought you were the worst kind of scheming female, I still couldn't let go."

"Oh, I'm so glad!" she said, going up on tiptoe to kiss him. "But I wasn't about to let you go, either, no matter what I had to do."

"Even if it meant fighting snakes!"

"Even then."

"And pushy big brothers."

"That, too."

"Or making love to me because you thought it was owed."

Her eyes widened and she went very still. "It's funny about that," she said. "When you were just a bunch of sweet letters and a prayer, I thought I could offer you that for making a home for the boys. It didn't seem so much then, but once I came to love you...."

"I know, honey," he said, pulling her up against him and holding her there. "I didn't want it that way, either."

"Good," she said, "because it won't ever be that way. I love you too much ever to let it be that way."

He chuckled. "Well, how about this way, then?" He pressed her against the barn door and kissed her, pouring his heart into it and plumbing her mouth with his tongue. By the time he stopped, they were both panting. "Oh, honey," he said, "please don't make me wait!"

She thought of his folks sitting up to breakfast in the house and of all the nights they'd wasted and she knew she'd never be able to answer him with anything but her heart. She laced her arms around his neck, and pressed her body against him, and nodded. He put his head back a moment in thanksgiving, then lifted her away from the barn door and carried her toward the room he'd shared with Newt.

"I've been thinking, Leon," she said softly against his throat. "I'd like to have another baby."

He stopped dead in his tracks, stunned, and then he started to laugh. "Why the hell not? What's one more at this point?"

She smiled and began to unbutton his shirt. "I sort of thought you might say that."

"Heck, I like kids. I might even like my own! Not that I don't consider our boys mine."

Our boys. She smiled, almost bursting with happiness. "I know. It's one of the reasons I love you and always will."

He stepped into the darkened room and gently laid her on the bed. "Well, if we're having babies now, I guess it's a good thing we'll have a space opening up in the fall."

She cocked her head, pulling at her shirttail. "How's that?"

He put his hands on his hips. "Our oldest is going off to college, and I don't want to hear any argument about it. He needs it. He deserves it. And I want him to have it."

She stared up at him for a long time, her eyes filling with tears of love and gratitude and joy, and then she lifted her hand in invitation. He didn't need another. He pulled the door closed and joined her. They came together unerringly, even in total darkness. For they would always find each other with their hearts.

*   *   *   *   *

Coming in August—

MONTANA MAVERICKS

*Twelve stories that capture living and loving
beneath the big sky.*

*Come to Whitehorn, Montana—where
the legend lives on—and the mystery
is just beginning. . . .*

*Here is an excerpt from
Rogue Stallion by Diana Palmer—
the first book in this exciting new series.*

One

Jessica Larson was fielding paperwork and phone calls with a calmness that she didn't feel. Since her promotion to social services director she'd become adept at presenting an unflappable appearance while having hysterics.

The perfunctory knock on her office door was followed by her secretary's high-pitched, "But she's busy...!"

"It's all right, Candy," Jessica called to the harassed young blonde. "I'm expecting McCallum." Although she hadn't expected him a half hour early. Sterling McCallum was a force of nature. He was like a wild stallion, a rogue stallion, who traveled alone and made his own rules. Secretly, she was awed by him.

McCallum didn't wait for her to ask him to sit down. He took the chair beside her desk and crossed one long leg over the other.

"Okay, what have you done with the child found on the Kincaid place?" he asked without preamble, looking utterably bored.

Jessica's gaze slid over his thick, dark hair to his equally dark eyes in an olive-tan face. He was big, although there was nothing remotely clumsy about him. He had a mouth she dreamed about: wide and sexy and definite. Broad shoulders tapered to narrow hips. He was so masculine he made her ache.

"Her name is Jennifer," she told him.

He glowered. "The abandoned baby."

Jessica gave up—for now. He would never treat a "case" as a person. Abandoned babies were exactly that. He allowed no one close to him. But Jessica knew he was vulnerable under that tough exterior. His childhood—an alcoholic mother and a series of foster homes after her death—was no secret to anyone in Whitehorn.

"All right, McCallum," she said, reaching for a file. "The baby was taken to Whitehorn Memorial. She's healthy and well cared for. We'll see her in the morning."

"I don't need to see it—"

"Her," she corrected. "Baby Jennifer."

"—to start searching for its parents," he concluded without missing a beat.

"We'll leave about nine," Jessica continued. "Don't be late. I need to catch up with all the work that never seems to get done."

McCallum stood to leave and Jessica followed him to the door. "Why don't you get married and let some strong man support you?" he taunted her.

She tilted her chin saucily. "Are you proposing, Deputy?" she asked with a wicked smile. "Has someone tantalized you with stories of my homemade bread?"

He'd meant it sarcastically, but she'd turned the tables on him neatly. He gave a reluctant grin.

"I'm not the marrying kind," he said. "I don't want a wife and kids."

Her bright expression dimmed a little, but the smile lingered. "Not everyone does," she said agreeably. The ringing telephone caught her attention. She turned away from McCallum. "Thanks for stopping by. I'll see you in the morning."

McCallum's gaze slid over her bowed head. After a minute he turned and walked out, closing the door behind him. He did it without a goodbye. Early in his life, he'd learned not to look back.

That night McCallum watched the neighborhood children ride by on bicycles. McCallum watched the kids as a stranger watches. He was answerable to no one, free to do whatever he pleased with no interference.

He'd had the flu last winter. He'd lain in bed for over twenty-four hours, burning with fever, unable to cook or even get into the kitchen. Not until he missed work did anyone look for him. It had punctuated how alone he really was.

He hadn't been alone long, though. As soon as she'd heard, Jessica had come over, ignoring his protests. She fed him and cleaned for him, and only left when he proved he could get out of bed. Since then he'd been ruder than ever to Jessica. When he'd gone back to work the other men had teased him about Jessica. He'd taken out that irritation on her.

He hadn't even thanked her for her trouble, he recalled. No matter how rude he was, she kept coming back. She was his one weakness, although, thank God, she didn't know it. He was curt because he had to keep her from knowing about his weakness. He had been doing a good job; when she looked at him these days, she never met his eyes.

At nine o'clock sharp, McCallum showed up in Jessica's office.

"We'll go in my car," he said. As they headed toward the parking lot, he slipped his sunglasses over his eyes. They gave him an even more threatening profile.

She hesitated, then let him help her into the car. She clasped her briefcase on her lap as they started off for the hospital. Glancing out the window, Jessica took in the beautiful spring day in Montana. The area around White-horn had rolling hills that ran forever. Occasional herds of cattle dotted the horizon. There were cottonwood and willow trees along the streams, but mostly the country was wide-open. It was home. She loved it.

The hospital wasn't far, and soon Jessica and Sterling were at the nursery. Baby Jennifer was in a crib. She looked very pretty, with big blue eyes and a tuft of blond hair. She looked up at her visitors without a change of expression, although her eyes were alert and intelligent.

Jessica looked at her hungrily. She put down her briefcase and after a questioning glance at the nurse, she picked up the baby and held her close.

"Little angel," she whispered, smiling so sadly that the man at her side scowled. She touched the tiny hand and felt it curl around her finger. She held back tears. She would never have a baby. She would never know the joy of feeling it grow in her body, watching its birth, nourishing it at her breast . . .

She made a sound and McCallum moved between her and the nurse with magnificent carelessness. "I want to see any articles of clothing that were found on or with the child," he said courteously.

The nurse, diverted, produced a small bundle and McCallum went through it carefully. He sighed. No clues to the child's parents here.

He was still frowning when he turned back to Jessica. She was just putting the child into her crib and straightening. The look on her face was all too easy to read, but she quickly concealed her thoughts with a businesslike expression.

Jessica told the nurse, "I'll need to speak to the attending physician."

"Of course, Miss Larson. If you'll come with me?"

McCallum followed the women as they went to Dr. Henderson's office. Jessica arranged for Jennifer's release the next morning.

"I'll send over the necessary forms," Jessica assured him, shaking hands.

"Pity, isn't it?" the doctor said sadly. "Throwing away a baby, like that."

"She wasn't exactly thrown away," Jessica reminded him. "At least she was left where people could find her."

They said their goodbyes and McCallum and Jessica walked toward the exit. He glanced down at her. "How old are you?"

"I'm twenty-five," she said. "Why?"

He looked ahead instead of at her, his hands stuck deep into his jean pockets. "These modern attitudes may work for some women, but they won't work for you. Why don't you get married and have babies of your own, instead of mooning over someone else's?"

She didn't answer him. Rage boiled up inside her, quickening her steps as they left the hospital. He had no right to make such remarks about her. Her private life was none of his business!

His keen eyes cut to her face. "You cried," he said shortly.

She grasped her briefcase like a lifeline, ignoring him. She was breathing through her nostrils. Her eyes were like brown coals, and she was livid.

"Your hand is itching, isn't it?" he taunted. "You want to hit me, but you can't work up the nerve."

"You have no right to talk to me like this!"

"How did you ever get into this line of work?" he demanded. "You're a bleeding heart liberal with more pity than purpose in your life. If you'd take down that hair and keep on those contact lenses, you might even find a man who'd marry you. Then you wouldn't have to spend your life burying your own needs in a job that's little more than a substitute for an adult relationship with a man!"

"You...!" The impact of the briefcase on his shoulder shocked him speechless. She hit him again before he could recover. It was leather and it was heavy, but it was the shock of the attack that left him frozen as she stalked off.

She started off down the street with her hair hanging in unruly strands from its once-neat bun, a rip in her hose and her jacket askew and wrinkled. She looked dignified even in her pathetic state, and she didn't look back once.

Dark secrets, dangerous desire...

Lovers
DARK AND
DANGEROUS

Three spine-tingling tales from the dark side
of love.

This October, enter the world of shadowy
romance as Silhouette presents the third in their
annual tradition of thrilling love stories and
chilling story lines. Written by three of
Silhouette's top names:

LINDSAY McKENNA
LEE KARR
RACHEL LEE

Haunting a store near you this October.

Only from

Silhouette®

...where passion lives.

Take 4 bestselling love stories FREE

Plus get a FREE surprise gift!

Special Limited-time Offer

Mail to Silhouette Reader Service®

> P.O. Box 609
> Fort Erie, Ontario
> L2A 5X3

YES! Please send me 4 free Silhouette Romance™ novels and my free surprise gift. Then send me 6 brand-new novels every month, which I will receive months before they appear in bookstores. Bill me at the low price of $2.50 each plus 25¢ delivery and GST*. That's the complete price and—compared to the cover prices of $3.25 each—quite a bargain! I understand that accepting the books and gift places me under no obligation ever to buy any books. I can always return a shipment and cancel at any time. Even if I never buy another book from Silhouette, the 4 free books and the surprise gift are mine to keep forever.

315 BPA AQS2

Name _____ (PLEASE PRINT)

Address _____ Apt. No. _____

City _____ Province _____ Postal Code _____

This offer is limited to one order per household and not valid to present Silhouette Romance™ subscribers. *Terms and prices are subject to change without notice. Canadian residents will be charged applicable provincial taxes and GST.

CSROM-694

©1990 Harlequin Enterprises Limited

MONTANA Mavericks

Stories that capture living and loving beneath the Big Sky, where legends live on...and the mystery is just beginning.

This September, look for

THE WIDOW AND THE RODEO MAN
by Jackie Merritt

And don't miss a minute of the loving as the mystery continues with:

SLEEPING WITH THE ENEMY
by Myrna Temte (October)
THE ONCE AND FUTURE WIFE
by Laurie Paige (November)
THE RANCHER TAKES A WIFE
by Jackie Merritt (December),
and many more!

Wait, there's more! Win a trip to a Montana mountain resort. For details, look for this month's MONTANA MAVERICKS title at your favorite retail outlet.

Only from **V** *Silhouette*® where passion lives.

Is the future what it's cracked up to be?

This August, find out how C. J. Clarke copes with being on her own in

GETTING IT TOGETHER: CJ
by Wendy Corsi Staub

Her diet was a flop. Her "beautiful" apartment was cramped. Her "glamour" job consisted of fetching coffee. And her love life was less than zero. But what C.J. didn't know was that things were about to get better....

The ups and downs of modern life continue with

GETTING IT RIGHT: JESSICA
by Carla Cassidy in September

GETTING REAL: CHRISTOPHER
by Kathryn Jensen in October

Get smart. Get into "The Loop!"

Only from ▼ *Silhouette*®

where passion lives.

Relive the romance... This September,
Harlequin and Silhouette are proud to bring you

by Request™

Marry Me... Again!

Some men are worth marrying *twice*...

Three complete novels by your favorite authors—
in one special collection!

FULLY INVOLVED by Rebecca Winters
FREE FALL by Jasmine Cresswell
MADE IN HEAVEN by Suzanne Simms

If you're looking to rekindle something wild, passionate
and unforgettable—then you're in luck.

Available wherever
Harlequin and Silhouette books are sold.

HARLEQUIN®   *Silhouette*®